The author wrote for primary school play *Cinderella and Mathematics*
2011

Participated as a volunteer writer in a youth club in Saudi Arabia.
2012

Published his first novel (*The Unique Copy*) in Arabic
2013

Published his second writing of stories collection – Love – was not accepted
2015

Attended a course (A professional writing narration) in the General Authority for Youth and Sports.
2017

Attended workshop (180 Media) in Youth Affairs Authority which was made in Kuwait, London and Manchester (BBC TV)
2018

Attended Public Relations Academy course.

Participated in the volunteer campaign the Syrian refugee children.

To my princesses, Alaa and Fajer
"We are full of hope and optimism and are moving toward love."
Your beloved mum

# Hawraa Albahrani

---

# THE TATTOO

A lot of realities in myths!

*To: Miss Mclaren*

*Enjoy reading*

*I hop you like my book*

*22.6 2023*

**AUSTIN MACAULEY PUBLISHERS™**
LONDON • CAMBRIDGE • NEW YORK • SHARJAH

Copyright © Hawraa Albahrani 2023

The right of Hawraa Albahrani to be identified as author of this work has been asserted by the author in accordance with sections 77 and 78 of the Copyright, Designs and Patents Act 1988.

All rights reserved. No part of this publication may be reproduced, stored in a retrieval system, or transmitted in any form or by any means, electronic, mechanical, photocopying, recording, or otherwise, without the prior permission of the publishers.

Any person who commits any unauthorised act in relation to this publication may be liable to criminal prosecution and civil claims for damages.

This is a work of fiction. Names, characters, businesses, places, events, locales, and incidents are either the products of the author's imagination or used in a fictitious manner. Any resemblance to actual persons, living or dead, or actual events is purely coincidental.

A CIP catalogue record for this title is available from the British Library.

ISBN 9781788786560 (Paperback)
ISBN 9781788788854 (ePub e-book)

www.austinmacauley.com

First Published 2023
Austin Macauley Publishers Ltd®
1 Canada Square
Canary Wharf
London
E14 5AA

I offer my sincere gratitude and appreciation to the heart of my father, who is still with me despite his death.

I would also like to take this opportunity to extend my sincere gratitude to my husband.

Abdulaziz for his strong confidence in my talent.

My gratitude and appreciation to Mr Mohamed Dagher who helped me in translation.

# Story 1

# A Lot of Realities in Myths!

The sun began to set, and the train was about to arrive, and despite the calmness of the place, my pregnant mother knew that I had some challenges the whole world could never face. My blue eyes were full of concerns and my seven-year-old heart was overwhelmed with fear and did not know what was going around. I decided to run away with mother from a danger awaiting us. I had a lot of questions and my eyes kept staring at the window.

The train arrived at Royal Inverness Station, the farthest point from our house. My mother got down from the car, holding my hands firmly in order not to be lost in the crowd. Someone hit my mother suddenly, but she discreetly cried in order not to draw attention. When we went out to the street, my mother held my hands strongly. Thus, my concern for my father was mixed up with fear of losing my mother. I asked about what happened to her at the station, but she replied that it was something I should have not worried about.

She reassured me, but I was not convinced, because what happened was really worrying. When I felt worried about my father, I used to catch the necklace he put around my neck yesterday. This helped me to feel that he was near me. We got on a taxi…

However, I was still surprised by my mother's calmness and cool reaction despite the horrible situation we faced yesterday. She preferred to run away despite hearing severe criticism about my father. "My father, how do you want me to be your hero and you are in stories as my superhero and beloved prince?"

While we were watching the TV, my father entered the house and his face was pale. He asked us to collect our stuff to leave the house as quickly as possible. Although, I rejected to leave my room, school and friends, he took me to my room upstairs and put this necklace around my neck. "I apologise for your childhood, but I need you to be my hero. Mira, you will face a new stage of your life. If you feel loneliness or difficulty, unlock the necklace and read my message," my father said.

With tears shedding from my eyes, I asked, "Why don't want to tell me now?"

He hugged me tenderly, saying, "Mum knows what I conceal from you."

Although, I did not understand him clearly, I cried loud while hugging him. Then, the door of our house was broken, so I felt afraid and hugged my father strongly to protect me from the coming thief. However, he did not protect or even reassure me for the first time. He delivered me to my mother who took me out from a hidden door in their room. Nobody saw us, and I took a step forward and then stopped to say, "I need my father."

However, my mother pulled me strongly without uttering a single word. She took me to the car that was parked in the backyard of our neighbour's house. I heard gunfire in our house and saw the glass of my room being shattered. I screamed loud, but my mother muffled my voice and whispered, "Get in the car; nobody should see us."

I looked at her with surprise, and said, "How is my father?"

"Get in the car! He will be OK," she replied.

I trusted her because she never lied to me. I did not believe my ears which heard the gunfire and my eyes which saw the glass being shattered.

Suddenly, my mother's voice ended my mind-wandering. We reached a small house in a narrow street with poor light. My mother whispered, "I hope this place is safe." However, I felt worried that we were still unsecured.

We entered the house which was somewhat clean, and someone was living in it. However, what drew my attention was that there was food in the fridge. We ate something and drank a cup of milk. Then, I went to bed in the room my mother selected for me upstairs, and she entered the next room. However, I was afraid and could not sleep. It was the first time in my life to feel this horror. I went to her room and knocked the door but was not surprised that she was still awake.

My mother was breathless and hugged me. I asked her, "Who are such people? What do they want from my father? Why are we unsecured?"

She hugged me strongly, saying, "You know that your father is a genetic engineering professor, and in his recent research, he has reached a genetic modification that can protect man from the harms of nuclear weapons. The idea of his research came in the first moments of your birth."

She added that my father promised to make a safe research for children who are the hope of future. He applied the research to animals, but there were some observations on the final result. For fear of exacerbation of the problem, the laboratory disposed of the genetically modified animal that was exposed to a nuclear weapon. After that day, your father received a call from an anonymous person asking him to sell the research for one billion, but your father refused for fear of human life because the results were not as he expected. We are being hunted since that night."

Staring at my mother's eyes, I asked, "What is the fate of my father?"

I saw despair in her eyes, and said, "He should give them the research and come back to us."

"This means that the whole world would die. The history will record him as a murderer rather than a professor," my mother replied.

I kept silent. Then, she said, "They already have the research after stealing it from the laboratory. However, they need the missing part."

Shaking my head, I asked, "How were these parts lost?"

"I told you that we are being chased from the moment your father refused to sell the research. He took precautions and hid the most important part of the research, so they won't be able to implement it," my mother replied.

I wished I were the foetus in her womb. I wished I had not seen my father or even liked him. I wished I had known him from the stories narrated by my mother. "Foetus, how lucky you are! You still have three months to come to this world. I hope I could exchange roles with you."

I hardly slept that night, and my sleep was accompanied by terrifying nightmares I had never had before.

My mother kissed me in the morning. Her face was pale, and I saw her smiling as if everything was going well. She said, "You have to accompany me. You will be enrolled today in a new school to start studying with your new colleagues," my mother said. However, I kept silent and did not reply to her. She said, "Mira, we should return to our normal life to bless your father when he comes back."

I did not intend to get up because of the concerns I was having, but as soon as she mentioned my father and what we would do to make him happy, I felt excited and prepared myself to go out while smiling dazzlingly. However, something stopped me in the centre of the room. "Mum, how would I go out with these clothes?" I asked my mother.

My clothes were dirty, my hair was not brushed, and my body was exhausted. I needed a hot shower. She opened the wardrobe in my room to find the clothes, shoes and toiletries I needed. I was surprised and could not even comment. "What is this house that is equipped with all of our needs?"

"This house was bought by your father after his research was stolen," she said while smiling tenderly. "Our escape to a distant point was part of the defence plan he prepared. He used to come here from time to time to prepare everything in anticipation of what happened today."

I laughed out loud because of the love which my father overwhelmed us with despite his absence. He not only took his precautions to save the world but also to keep our presence in his absence. What I knew about my father made me feel that he was with us, and anxiety faded when I went out with my mother.

While submitting my documents to the new school, my mother talked with the principal about some details. I kept looking at student pictures which were hanged on the wall. Meanwhile, I surrendered to the grief of leaving my friends. I decided not to love anyone in this school so as not to suffer parting or missing him when my circumstances would force me to leave the school. Suddenly, I heard my mother calling and felt that something was bothering her. She approached and asked me, "Mira, what was your father's name?"

I kept staring at her and feeling nauseous from the shock. I said with a trembling voice, "Are you kidding? How can you forget my father's name?" I swear she was confused and her face was pale. I believed her excuse but did not believe my eyes for the second time.

The principal intervened. "My sweetie, this is one of the symptoms of pregnancy in the last months; don't worry about Mum."

The principal's words were as a lifeline for my mother. "Yes, the memory is affected by pregnancy. You will be a mum one day and will remember my words." She was smiling tremblingly while looking at my eyes.

After leaving the school, my mother told me that our next destination is the market to buy new clothes for the school. I liked marketing so much, and I decided to buy some toys especially as I knew that my mother would not refuse.

The mall was not that large, and we bought our stuff as quickly as possible. However, something strange happened this time; my mother took the shopping bag without paying the bill. The accountant screamed loud. I said, "Mum, you forced us into an awkward position. How would you take the bag without paying the bill?"

My mother looked at me coldheartedly. The mall guard approached, saying, "You can't take the bag without paying the bill."

People gathered around us, saying, "We will help you if you don't have enough money."...What an embarrassing situation!

Suddenly, my mother held her head, saying, "Sorry, I was absent-minded. I apologise and will pay now."

"Mum, you were not absent-minded; you left me alone and went to another place...what happened to you?" I whispered.

After paying the bill, my mother apologised and said, "Would you mind selling a new toy for you?"

"Why should I believe your justification and don't believe my eyes, nose and feelings? Anyway, I am happy that you are still with me, and didn't mind selling a new toy to me," I said while holding her hands firmly.

While going home, I said, "Why don't we buy a car instead of the one we left near the train station? Why do we ride the train instead of the car?"

"This is better for us because someone would monitor the car or even install a GPS in it. I think the train was safe for us. There is a car in the garage of the house where we live. We will wash it and then start riding it. Your father prepared everything for us," my mother replied.

I hugged her and said, "I love you and Dad so much. I am very hungry, can we eat something?"

"I am also hungry. Let's go ahead!" she replied.

We went to a snack restaurant. It was very quiet, and my mother ordered a dish of spaghetti macaroni. I hit my face with my little hands out of surprise, and said, "Mum, we are in a restaurant offering snacks and not Italian food."

The waiter was confused, and my mother kept staring at me. I ordered two sandwiches of hamburger on her behalf.

I looked at her and took money from her wallet to pay the bill. I felt that my mother was starting to forget again. Before she talked, I said, "I know that Mum's memory is affected by pregnancy."

She smiled and said, "No, this might be because I did not sleep yesterday. I feel sleepy." I smiled for this convincing justification. My mind believed it but my heart did not. I felt that my mother was not fine, but I did not believe this feeling and said to myself that my mother never lied to me.

The calmness I felt was mixed with the hope that my father would return to us.

I kept silent at the school for about two or three weeks. The place was boring for me. I wanted to make new friends, but I was afraid that I would leave them without having the chance to bid farewell. I was worried about my mother's health. Her memory was not good, and I did not know what to do. The only thing that occupied my mind during the academic day was how to take care of my pregnant mother.

A few days later, I felt comfortable at the school and it became a safe place for me. My classmate Noah used to come with his lunch and sit in front of me after he had noticed that I usually sit in the corner alone. "Hey, I hear you!" he said. I did not pay him any attention or even utter a single word in the beginning. He did the same thing for almost two weeks and did not feel tired.

Then, I smiled because of his insistence and said, "Didn't get tired?"

"Why should I get tired?" he asked.

"You sit in front of me at the same time and the same place for three weeks. You said that you heard me though I did not utter a single word," I replied.

He laughed and I was amazed at his laugh, saying, "I don't make a joke."

He said, "Sorry, but you said that I hear you despite your silence. Don't you talk with me now? Sitting in front of you for three weeks was useful."

I smiled shyly and found out that Noah was right. He managed to get me out of silence. I liked to talk with him as I wished to make new friends.

Meeting this friend reminded me of my father's words – "after hardships comes ease". Noah became the loveliest thing I had after moving to Inverness. He helped me to get out of silence and accept everything new in my life. He did not only want to know the secrets of my life but also tried to get me out of my loneliness. I liked school so much because it was a place where I met new friends. I did not remember when or how I unveiled my secrets to Noah, but I admitted that I felt comfortable when I revealed my concerns to him. He promised to keep my secrets and help me whenever I needed that. I used to say, "Noah, I will not tell you anything unless you promise to help me."

However, my request did not last long. I came to him before entering the classroom and asked to talk with him. I said, "Noah, I am worried about Mum, and don't know how to behave."

He looked at me with a surprise, saying, "What's wrong? Anyone attacked you?"

I replied in negative, and said, "While having lunch yesterday, Mum complained about the movement of foetus, and shouted loud. I reassured her that this was her second pregnancy, and she shouldn't feel worried about anything. However, what broke my heart was her question about the first child. Mum doesn't remember that I am her first child." I then cried loud.

Noah tried to calm me down, but I could not stop crying. I told him that I could not sleep the whole night because of my sadness. "What increases my sadness is that when I feel that I am in need of my father, I remember his apology for my childhood." I kept crying and Noah kept looking at me. He did not know how to help me.

My enthusiasm for study had faded away and I began to hate my life. My mother's health got even worse, and we did not hear anything about my father since he left us. However, I got used to her forgetfulness, and became reassured about her especially when she regained her consciousness.

I was extremely worried at the end of the academic day when I found myself alone. I then said, "Mum hasn't come."

"Have they come to her?"

"Has she forgotten me?"

"What is my fate?"

When my concerns increased, I phoned my mother from the school office. She thought that I was in my room. Her voice was free from worries but full of forgetfulness. I then asked myself, "Didn't Mum think of me?"

Within ten minutes, she arrived at the school and apologised to me. While driving home, she kept looking at me, waiting for me to comment. I said, "Mum, this forgetfulness is not because of pregnancy or fatigue. There is something strange happening to you. I believe my concerns."

She held my hand and looked at me as serious as she used to do when she wanted to reveal something beyond my stamina. My mother started to complain about her concern and forgot that I was her child and not her friend.

She said with a trembling voice: "In fact, I don't like to go to a specialist as he would unveil our issue and pursue us again. When the bout of forgetfulness comes, I suffer from pain on the side I was struck at when I was at the train station. I also suffer from headache which ends with the recovery of my consciousness. I feel that I don't forget as much as I go unconscious."

I asked her while crying, "Does this mean that what happened at the moment of arrival was intentional and not by mistake?"

She replied in positive, saying, "This means that we are being hunted from the moment we left the house."

I kept silent but started to feel worried again.

At this moment, I hoped that tomorrow would come in order to meet Noah and talk with him about my concerns. I then asked myself, "Will the one pursuing us wait for tomorrow?"

We reached the house and found the door open. The place was a mess, so we knew that someone was looking for something.

My mother held my little hands and left the house as if a lion would prey on us. We got in the car, and my mother drove madly. I was afraid because she was not healthily qualified to drive fast. "Where are we going?" I asked.

She replied, "I don't know." I asked her to drive slowly, but she shouted at me and asked to keep silent. After an hour of driving, she stopped the car in a public parking. We got in a taxi which took us to a far rural house.

Again, I left lovely memories behind even my friend who did not know when I would come back. I should have adapted to life in this new house amidst fields and away from noise and eyes.

My mother asked the taxi driver to stop in the middle of the road, and then we walked home. I asked her, "I started to feel tired of walking. Why didn't you ask him to drive us home?"

"I was afraid he would be a spy. This is to ensure our safety," my mother replied.

We knocked on the door with a new hope. It was a small house located behind a farm where some pets such as sheep and chickens live. I thought we heard the sound of a horse there. An aged lady opened the door and welcomed us with a smile. The lady with short grey hair was wearing cotton clothes, a knitted sweater and glasses. She looked like the grandma whose story was narrated in novels. I almost thought she was had come out of a novel.

I did not like her in the beginning and hid myself behind my mother. Although she received us warmly, I did not want to stay here for long. I did not want to like someone and then leave him because of my tough conditions. I was amazed at her tenderness and care towards my mother. I later knew that she would be the midwife of my mother.

She tried to get closer to me through narrating some stories before sleep and preparing my favorite food. In addition, she asked me to help her on the farm. Although the work was easy, she asked me to help her in order to get me out of my silence. She also offered us some clothes. Though such clothes were old, they were still good. I started to get worried about her because those pursuing us may hurt this old lady for taking care of my mother. I hoped that my mother would give birth to a boy so I would remain the sole daughter of my father. This was my way of thinking at this little age.

I enjoyed the quietness of this rural life as well as working on the farm with my hands. I also enjoyed playing with pets on the farm as they were overflowing with compassion. I even felt that their sound was like music and in harmony with nature. I saw sheep and chickens as weak as my mother who were suffering from bouts of forgetfulness or unconsciousness.

"What did they do to you, Mum?"

She forgot things, memories and events as well as her most significant needs, and became in need of someone to help her as if she was a one-year-old child. This happened one month after living in this house. My mother was in her nine month of pregnancy. I washed my hands to have lunch since I was very hungry. Playing with sheep drained my energy out. Suddenly, I heard my mother screaming. She was burnt by hot food which fell on her clothes. I noticed that my mother's hand was trembling, and heard the old lady saying, "It seems that your condition is getting worse."

I asked her, "What do you mean that her condition is getting worse?"

She told me that my mother was suffering from Alzheimer's.

"What does Alzheimer's mean?" I asked the old lady.

She said the symptoms of this disease include forgetting simple things, and then the daily tasks. Finally, the patient would face difficulty in movement. I did not understand her but was sure that this would be the reason behind my mother's suffering.

In the beginning, I thought that taking care of my mother was more interesting than going to school. I used to ask her every two minutes, "Are you hungry?" She would laugh pleasantly. However, the old lady did not allow me to feed my mother as she saw her crying when I was feeding her. I understood the tragedy of the moment. I lost my mother's interaction with me and missed her laughing and joking.

How can I imagine the idea of not feeding my mother with my little hands? She used to fulfill all of my needs. She was my world in which I sought refuge from enemies. My heart broke like a dish on the ground, when I saw her in need of help to get into the toilet. My mother was hardly moving so the old lady came to help her. "Mum, I hope you are fine," I said.

When I was her unable to do something, I wondered what else she would lose. I could not believe that the situation would get worse. The enemies did not only make my mother forget me and her pregnancy, but also made her unable to feed herself. They also managed to make her unable to enter the toilet. My mother's health got worse to the extent that she forgot the pain of delivery. I could not tell her that her bouts of forgetfulness hurt me.

One night, the old lady brought the dinner early, saying, "You are going to eat alone because your mother is suffering from the pains of delivery. We have to be ready for receiving the baby."

Then, she left me and went upstairs. I did not eat and kept worried until I heard the cries of my mother. I could not endure her crying. The old lady stood on the ladder and looked at me. I left the dining table and sat on the ladder. She laughed and said, "Don't worry, why crying?" Then, she went away.

I remember those moments very well. I prayed for my mother with all my heart, asking Allah to bless her and return my father safely to us. At almost midnight, I heard pure angelic cries from inside the room.

I rushed up to see the little boy being rolled by the old lady in a white cloth. I smiled and my eyes were full of tears. She said, "You have a pretty sister like you now."

I kissed my sister's forehead although her face was dirty. I hoped this baby would be a male, but I liked her so much, anyway. I thanked God that my mother did not need to go the hospital because if we moved to the hospital, the enemies would have caught us there. I looked at my mother and saw her eyes closed. The old lady reassured me, saying, "Do not worry, she is just asleep."

I approached her, kissed her head and wiped sweat from her forehead. She opened her eyes and smiled, saying, "I hear the cries of a baby. Do we have a guest?" Her words let me lose any hope that she would recover soon.

"How can I answer, Mum?"

I looked at her, put my little hands on her belly, and said, "She is your little baby. Don't remember the severe pains of delivery?"

I saw the tears shedding from her eyes with surrender as if she was my child. She said, "I can hardly remember you, my sweetie. If what you say is right, please try to be as a mum to your sister. It seems that my condition is getting worse."

The old lady showered the baby, put her on her mother's chest, and then asked me to go out as they needed to relax.

However, I was extremely worried that night. The old lady woke me up at dawn calmly. She then took me and my little sister to the kitchen and put us in a large waste container. She covered us with garbage and waste bags. Before asking or even opposing, she said, "Don't go out of the container under any circumstances. It is better to sleep. Take care of your little sister."

I remembered that I heard the same words and experienced the same worries before. It seemed that the enemies were looking for us and the old lady knew something about them. I then asked myself, "Will she betray Mum? Is she with or against us? I hope that Father is living with us now."

I sat where she ordered me and closed my eyes in order to sleep, but I hoped to wake up from that nightmare. I hoped to open my eyes to find myself living with my mother and father together in one house. I hoped to open my eyes to see my mother and her baby in the hospital and not in a rural house. I hoped to buy toys for my little sister and open my eyes to find everything different.

I did not know if I had slept or went unconscious because of this stink. I do not remember the situation well, but I think that I heard some people fighting. I said, "It seems that everything is over. I will get out of this container in which the old lady asked me to sit." However, the crying of my sister while trying to get up refreshed my memory that was affected by fatigue. I stopped for a moment to think, and then doubted that someone broke into the house, so the old lady hid us there. I clutched the baby to my chest and did not know if I could do that that or not. I tried to behave like a mother as requested by our lovely mother.

I got out of the container and was not surprised by the chaos in the place. I called my mother and the old lady with a frightened voice, but no one answered. I went upstairs and breathed a sigh of relief when I found her sitting on the chair facing the window. This was her favorite place for sewing.

"I thought that something wrong happened to you. Why didn't you get me out of the garbage?" However, I approached to find her shot in the head.

I hugged my little sister and kept silent. Then, I started looking for my mother, saying, "If they killed this poor old lady, what would they have done to Mum?"

For the first time, I wished that they would have taken my mother with them rather than killing her. I knew that I could not see her shot, so I preferred death to seeing her killed. I broke into the room and found her soaked with blood. They fired three shots at her chest. I approached her calmly in order to not disturb her if she was still alive.

I approached and put my little sister on her chest to get compassion. The baby was crying loudly so I whispered in my mother's ears, "Mum, look! My sister is hungry. Will you breastfeed her?"

My mother did not answer me. I screamed and put her hand on my chest. Both me and my little sister kept crying loud. I screamed for the parting of my father as well as the death of my mother and the poor lady. I was afraid of the unknown future awaiting us.

I blamed my mother, saying, "How could you leave me in such simple way? You offered me toys but did not tell me that you would give me something that was not a toy. You left me a soul without training me how to take care of it. Mum, I still need someone to take care of me…"

For the first time, my mother did not answer me. She used to answer even when she was unconscious. I took my little sister and slept with our mother under one cover. We sometimes cried and sometimes kept silent. I sometimes blamed and sometimes bit my fingers in order to not disturb my sister by crying. The more my mother kept silent, the more I needed her hug. I closed my eyes and wished to die like her.

I slept next to my mother for long time. I felt disappointed for not dying like her but it seemed that I just slept. I stood up hardly to look from the window. I found that the sun was setting in preparation for a new day. "My God, I lost hope, and became alone in this world. I had a little sister who needs Mum more than life." I then asked myself, "How could I stop days? How could I delay sunset? How could I stop time in order to not to leave Mum?"

Then, I started to feel the coldness of the corpse, and noticed that her arms turned blue. I swallowed my saliva and got afraid of Mum and saw her as a ghost for the first time. Her countenances were changed due to the effect of blood. Anyway, she became a dead body.

I wore my shoes and took additional cover for the baby. I lifted her from my mother's chest and clutched her to my trembling chest. I went out in the dark, not knowing how or where to go. I only wanted to run away.

I walked for a long distance at midnight and the little baby was sleeping quietly.

My god, help me!!!

I felt tired from walking and hid myself behind the trees overlooking the main street. I slept a little, and then woke up when I heard the sound of a car that was parked next to me. I then asked myself, "Did someone see me? Who is he? How could I run away from him?"

I heard someone having a call. "Dawn approached, why worry? Well, I will reach Loch Ness at sunrise…Prepare breakfast, my friend."

The man ended the call and walked around the car. He seemed to be tired from driving for long hours so he did some exercises and then turned on the engine and drove away.

I entered the trunk without allowing him to see me. The word 'Loch Ness' reminded me of the stories my father used to narrate to me before sleeping. I was eager to see the place of legends with my own eyes. None of the enemies would think that I might be there.

As the sun was about to rise, my sister woke up and started to cry. I put my little finger in her mouth as if it was my mother's breast. The man doubted that someone was riding with him, so he decided to raise the sound of music to dispel such illusion.

When we reached the lake, I quietly got off, thanking God that I had arrived peacefully. When I looked at the lake, the beauty of the place captured me. Both I and my sister cried loud. Tears kept shedding and I hoped to erase the image of seeing my mother and the old lady killed with these tears. I kept breathing cold air strongly to forget the smell of blood. I then said, "Nature, I came to you alone. Can you hug me? Don't let me and sister go back."

I sat on the green grass quietly. When I saw visitors and tourists there, I felt disappointed, and then asked, "Why should I be deprived of my father and mother? Is it a crime to have a father working in the field of researches? Why is evil always the strongest party in stories?"

In the noon, my sister cried loud because of hunger. I asked myself, "What should I do?" I did not even have milk. Even if I had it, I did not know how to prepare it. I had only one way to solve this problem without drawing attention that I was a child without care.

I did not want to steal and did not imagine that I would be a thief one day. But what should I do to feed this hungry baby? I turned around and saw a beautiful family with a baby carriage. There was a baby bottle hanging from the bag. I approached with my heart pulse accelerating. I then extended my trembling hands in the child's bag, and took the bottle. The family was busy taking photos and meditating at the place was like a painting designed with love. I took the prepared milk, and my tears were shedding with apology. I swear I was forced to commit such an ugly act. Now I knew why my mother starved to feed me. For the first time, I saw myself enduring hunger and thirst as my main concern was how to feed my sister.

I took the milk and ran away to the tree standing near the lake. I then sat to feed my sister.

We remained there until the sun was about to set. "O sun, will you set and leave me with the darkness again?" The last ship in the lake moved, and people got in their cars, leaving me and the nature mother alone.

It was lull and calm at the same time, and I did not know what to do in this darkness. I carried the baby, hid in the castle and took shelter with the dead rocks that were gentler to me than human beings. The moon has not appeared that night. I closed my eyes and tried to warm myself because it was very cold. My sister sometimes slept, and sometimes played with the emptiness. When she screamed out of hunger, I used to put my finger in her mouth. But her voice rose, and this trick did not work anymore. I filled the empty bottle with water from the lake, but it fell from my hand and disappeared in the bottom because my hands were very cold and failed to hold the bottle firmly. I returned slowly to my sister while she was crying behind the stones. I sat and cried with her.

We stopped crying after hearing such horrible sound that emanated from the crash of something with the water. I was worried about my sister so I covered her with my cloth. It was a breathtaking moment, and then everything calmed down again. I considered this warm place was like my mother's chest. After hearing this wound, I stood up, stuck to rocks and stared at the lake.

I saw something strange. It was a terrifying huge creature swimming in the lake. I tried to identify its countenances but failed. It was not a dragon, dinosaur or even a giant bird, although he had two wings of diamonds illuminating the place magically despite the absence of the moon. "Is this the myth Dad was telling me about?" I asked myself. "Is this real?"

This creature was swimming in the lake circularly. It sometimes stretched its wings, glowing the lake, and sometimes pulled them back. It was something pretty that took my heart. I approached it bravely. The creature was not wilder than those people who were chasing me.

I got the little baby out of my clothes especially as her cry drew its attention. It came closer to me, but fear forced me to move away. The wild creature approached fast with its giant face. My body and hair surrendered to its strong breath that was like the wind. I lost my footing as it kept looking at me for long. I thought it was amazed by my presence there. Although its eyes were horrible, I did not move. I hope to be the princess that would be saved by this monster.

I brought my sister nearer to its face, and said, "This two-day-old baby is hungry and I have nothing to feed her."

The monster raised its head, so I felt disappointed. It then started to make a disturbing voice. I smiled unwillingly until I saw a giant bird flying in the sky. It was as big as our house. I did not know from where it came. However, it lied on the grass next to me, showing its udder. I saw it surrendering peacefully.

Without thinking, I brought my sister nearer to it, and helped her to feed from the udder. I smiled for the quietness of the place. My sister slept and I thanked the bird with its gentleness. It flew away, and the lake monster was still looking at me. I thanked it with the belief of a little child that it understood me. I then saw it disappearing in the darkness of the lake. I slept that night behind the rocks peacefully as if I were sleeping in my room.

It was strange to feel secured among such wild animals and unsecured among the humans.

I stayed by the lake for three days, receiving gifts and snacks from visitors in return for doing some work for them. My sister kept feeding from the bird every night and then slept quietly for long hours. On the fourth day, I woke up after having a strange dream. I dreamt of my mother saying, "Mira, take the infant and leave Loch Ness." I was struck by this dream in which my mother asked me to leave that quiet place although the baby was fine. However, I remembered my father's advice when he asked me to believe in the messages conveyed to us through dreams. I did not know whether I should believe this dream and leave the lake or not? I was living quietly at that place.

I did not intend to leave the lake, but I kept thinking of the dream and my mother's advice. I continued to perform my daily work but was stopped by an aged lady. I tried to see in her face the countenances of a kind grandmother but failed. She asked me to help her in return for offering me a delicious meal. I did not find any reason to refuse her offer. I noticed that she was trying to approach me and hold my hand, but I moved away from her. She asked to carry my sister but I refused firmly. When I approached the car, I found that it was equipped with a seat for the infant and another one for me. Without thinking, I ran fast while clutching the baby strongly. She pursued me, pulled my shirt and uncovered my shoulder. I shouted, "Help!"

Finally, I managed to escape and got on a bus. She was astonished about something, but I did not care. Anyway, I sat on the last seat next to an aged man who was asleep. All people thought that I was her daughter. "Where is my father to protect me from such cursed people? Where should I go now? The only safest place became unsecured."

I was breathing fast and my heart pulse was accelerating. I put my hand on my chest in order to reassure myself. I touched the necklace which my father gave me and remembered his advice. This was the worst situation I ever faced. I unlocked the necklace and found a piece of paper and some money. I found a message written by my father so I cried out of longing for him. I did not know if the message was still having his smell or this was just a delusion.

The message read: 'Mira, my little daughter, you are not alone; mine and your mother's hearts are with you. You are now at Inverness or near it. Go to the address written on the back of the paper and meet Mr Murdin who will help you. Sincerely, your beloved dad.'

I flipped it over and found the address. I held back tears in order to not to draw attention. "Dad, where would you take me?"

Fortunately, the bus of tourists stopped in downtown where Mr Murdin was living. I took a taxi and headed to his house. "Where is Mum?" the driver asked. "Why do you carry the baby? Don't you have a carriage for him?"

I took a deep breath as my mother used to do when she was confused by a question. I then said, "This is a girl."

He smiled but I did not feel well about this smile. He looked as if he was thinking of something. I thought he would report to the police. My heart was pulsing strongly out of fear. I doubted that this man would not let things go well. When we stopped at the traffic signal, I threw money on the seat, opened the door and ran fast. I did not look behind to see him, but I heard him shouting, "I will report the concerned authorities."

However, I kept running to hide myself among the crowd. I felt tired because I did not eat something since the morning. I threw all money in the taxi although this arrogant man deserved nothing. I continued my way to Mr Murdin. I asked a young man about the address, he smiled brightly as if he was a story prince. He said, "Mr Murdin, raise your head!" He pointed to the sign hanging on the wall behind me.

It was the tattoo shop of Mr Murdin. I arrived at the shop but did not know that it belonged to Mr Murdin. I smiled at this man and thanked him. Then I entered the shop and a weak girl with red hair received me. I did not know whether she was amazed by my presence or not. However, I did not care about her, and said, "Can I meet Mr Murdin?"

She looked at me with disgust, and then picked up the phone, saying, "There is a child wanting to meet you." Before she hanged up the phone, I had seen a man smiling and standing before me. He was not as beautiful as my father. I did not like the tattoos spread everywhere on his body, but I was reassured because he was my father's friend.

He said enthusiastically, "Are you Mira?"

I nodded my head in positive. He approached and pampered my little sister. "How pretty she is! She is a girl. Is she not?" he asked.

I nodded again. He said, "Follow me, please!" Then, he asked the thin girl to call Jane to complete his work as he would hold an urgent meeting.

I did not know why she was looking at me again with disgust, but I did not care anyway.

I followed Mr Murdin to his private office that was very small. He brought me a chair to sit on and took my little baby and put her on the bed that was like that of the hospital. Before sitting, he heard my stomach sound. He smiled tenderly, and I smiled shyly.

"It is better to be hungry; this will help us finish our work easily. Then, I will offer you a delicious meal," he said.

I looked at him and did not understand anything. He asked if my father sent me to him, so I shook my head and did not utter a single letter. I did not know why I was silent.

He said, "My little girl, listen to me! You are a hero because you managed to survive this long without unlocking the necklace. I thought I could meet you earlier. Your father was my closest friend, and he brought you between his arms to my office as you are doing now with your sister. Then, he asked me to draw a tattoo on your back. However, I was amazed because your father was against the idea of harming oneself. I asked him about the reason. Your father then told me about his research and those pursuing him, and confirmed that his research would be stolen, so he brought you here and asked me to draw a tattoo on your back."

I was amazed when I heard that. I did not know that I had a tattoo drawn on my back; thus, my mother did not allow me to wear open back clothes. I asked him, "Can I see that tattoo?"

Immediately, he brought two mirrors, uncovered my back and let me see the tattoo. It was liked intertwined symbols which I could not understand. I was extremely surprised about the tattoo I saw in the mirror. I knew where to find the missing part of the research. I said, "My situation became more dangerous."

He smiled and said, "Don't worry, your father phoned me almost nine months ago to tell me that your mother was pregnant. He asked me to transfer the tattoo to the coming baby. Your father phoned me at that night to tell me that he would leave a piece of paper with you until he comes to draw the tattoo on the awaited baby. Since then, your father hasn't come, and I didn't hear anything about him. Thus, I was waiting for you to come."

I shed tears and felt the care of my father. I said, "Okay, I am ready."

He took me to another room which was as small as the office. It had a bed like that of the hospital and some machinery that I never saw before. He asked me to sleep on the bed, and said, "You will be fully anaesthetised. Then, we will draw the tattoo on her back and remove it from yours. It will just take two or three hours."

I asked in a frightened voice, "Will everything be okay?"

He smiled and said, "Trust me!"

One hour…

Two…

Maybe more…I did not know.

I did not remember when I closed my eyes after asking me to trust him. I went unconscious. I tried to raise my head, and saw my little sister sleeping on a bed next to mine. I was reassured by her presence. Again I put my head on the pillow and closed my eyes.

"Mira…Mira! Are you okay?"

I opened my eyes to find Mr Murdin smiling when he saw me getting up.

He sat on a nearby chair and said, "I was worried about your slumber; your little sister woke up hours before you."

I lifted my head to reassure her presence, but I did not find her. Before shouting and looking for her, he said, "Don't worry, she is with the secretariat in the other room to feed her, change the diaper and dress her in heavy clothes because it is very cold."

I looked at him, with my tears shedding silently. I smiled and thanked him but did not know how to express my feeling. Mr Murdin approached me and wiped my tears tenderly. He asked me not to be worried about the future as everything would be fine. I tried to calm down as what they were looking for became no longer available with me.

Mr Murdin noticed my distraction, so he brought two mirrors and said, "Hey, look at your back! The research is no longer on your back."

It was like magic as the tattoo was completely removed from my back. That weak girl entered, and I saw her smiling for the first time. She said while carrying my sister, "The baby is fine now."

My sister was sleeping deeply between her hands. I said to my sister, "Sorry, I don't know how to carry you properly."

The girl then asked me, "What is the name of your sister?"

I was amazed at her question, and said, "I really don't know; I didn't think of naming her."

Mr Murdin laughed and said, "Put the infant on the bed, and then go out please."

The secretariat went out and we became alone again. "It is natural that you didn't think of naming her. Your father wanted to name her Eva."

Without any hesitation, I said, "No problem, I will name her Eva as my father wanted."

Mr Murdin smiled as if he wanted to say something. He said, "Mira, my little girl, you have to do with your sister what your father did with you."

I was astonished at his words, and then he said, "You have to leave a message in a necklace to your sister. You don't know what would happen tomorrow, and she would be alone someday. So you should help her understand what would happen around her."

My eyes blurred with tears. He said, "You became part of this war, and you should complete it. Leave tears and sadness alone."

I nodded in agreement of his advice. He brought a piece of paper and a pen from his pocket. I thought I would not be able to write and express my feelings, but I found that my hand was writing smoothly. When I ended and folded the paper, I felt that I would leave my sister someday. Mr Murdin took the paper and put it in the necklace, and then helped me get up. I walked to my sister, put the necklace around her neck and whispered in her ears, "My lovely Eva, I apologise for your childhood."

Mr Murdin then asked, "What will you do now?"

I smiled and told him that I had to leave the city because of feeling unsecured. "I need to go back to the lake." He wondered about my plan to go back to the lake where I did not have a house. I said, "It is enough for me that I feel secured there." I did not tell him about the lake monster in order to avoid being accused of madness.

He said, "No problem, you should have a delicious meal before leaving the place."

I smiled and thanked him for his help and tenderness. He joked, "So I will be the hero of a two-princess story."

I laughed loud unwillingly.

# How Many Hearts Were Terrified by Their Peers?

I bid farewell to Mr Murdin warmly, and then hugged my little sister to leave the place. This was few minutes before sunset. It was slightly cold, but I was reassured for my sister because she was wearing heavy clothes. Before leaving, Mr Murdin offered me a warm coat where I found money that would help me get a taxi to the lake in late hour. When I wore the coat and found the money in the pocket, I looked at him with astonishment. His face sparkled with smile as if he was my father. I hugged him strongly and thanked greatly.

While crossing the street, I tried to keep the smile made by Mr Murdin but someone caught my hand. In the beginning, I thought that the signal was red and I would cross the street with my distraction. I saw all people crossing, but I was moving backward.

It was a hand pulling me backward. "What should I do, my God?"

Immediately, I bit this lousy hand that caught me and fled to the nearest car to ride. I looked from the window to see this person. It was a man standing with the woman who was pursuing me at the lake. I became sure that it was a gang trying to catch me in order to threaten my father. "Don't worry, everything will be fine, Dad," I whispered.

On my way to the lake, I was extremely worried – but this time – about my sister. I then asked, "Where should I hide her?" My cards were on the table and the lake became no longer secured. I looked behind to find fear pursuing us. It was a big black car chasing mine.

I tried to control myself in order to not draw attention of the driver who said, "Are you afraid of anyone?"

I shook my head.

"Where is your father?" he asked.

I said, "I am going to him."

I kept silent but was worried about his silence. I was sure that he did not trust me, especially after he held his phone. I was afraid lest he should report me to the police before trying to hide my sister. Then, I doubted that he would be a member of the gang and would not drive me to the lake. The taxi stopped at the crossway, awaiting a large vehicle to pass. I seized this opportunity, opened the door and ran fast towards the lake which was almost nearby. I was running madly while clutching my little sister. I took off my shoes in the car in order to able to run as fast as I could. I did not look back, but was asking myself, "Will they pursue me on foot or by car? Will they shoot me? Will they catch me?"

I just knew that the lake was very nearby.

I could not take my breath, or even swallow my saliva. I started to lose my footing but was insistent on completing the mission I started.

I crossed the soft grass with my barefoot, and reached the passage running to the lake. I tried to take my breath to shout for help.

In seconds, I looked behind to see ten men with this cursed lady surrounding the place. All of them were awaiting a clarification for my presence at this place and shouting in the darkness.

I shouted three consecutive times but the lake monster did not respond as usual. The bird also did not appear to feed my hungry sister. I did not believe what happened. "I stayed with the monster and bird three consecutive days; they are real."

I was extremely shocked, looking at such men and the lake. I then said, "I will not abandon my father and mother's hopes and will not waste their sacrifices." My breath was accelerating, and suddenly felt as if I was suffocated.

The men were coming slowly towards me. I saw their countenances clearly when they approached me. I finally decided to throw myself and sister in the lake in order to make them feel disappointed at losing the last opportunity.

When I started to throw myself in the lake, one of them caught me. I felt that my feet did not touch the ground so I shouted again, hoping that this nightmare would end soon. I heard the terrifying sound I used to hear every night from the lake. The lake monster came out of the lake with its frightened sound, and the giant bird appeared to respond to my shout.

The men felt afraid and the person who was catching me ran away. I raised my sister towards the bird so it held her with its claws and disappeared in the darkness. The monster also disappeared in the water after stretching its diamond wings magically to brighten amidst the darkness.

I smiled out of triumph and happiness. However, I apologised for my sister as I could not see her once again, but I was sure that she became secured. After bidding her farewell, I surrendered to fatigue and tiredness. Then, I lost my consciousness.

I opened my eyes to feel a big difference between this moment and the other when I was with Mr Murdin. I did not know how long I was unconscious. I was hardly able to move my hands as I found my hands and legs chained with a bed.

I woke up earlier but tried not to make noise in order to not draw their attention. I hated them and did not want to talk with them. I was surrounded in the room with ten men and the cursed lady. Not one of them thought of unlocking the chains.

Their gangster asked seriously, "Where is the missing part of the research?"

I said, "I want to meet my dad."

He smiled sarcastically, "The missing part is in return for your dad."

I turned my face away from him, saying, "I don't know its place."

He turned my face as tough as I thought my neck was broken. Then, he shouted, "You are a liar, your dad told me that you have the missing part. He told me before all of them that the missing part is with Mira."

I hit him with the steel I had in my hand angrily, and shouted, "You are a liar. Let me see Dad to prove the opposite is true."

The men held their gangster back in order to not to hit me. He threatened to deprive me of food and drink, and that I would bear the result of hitting him. However, I kept silent and did not care for his threat. The old lady changed my sitting position fast without taking into consideration that I was chained. She uncovered part of my back, and said angrily, "How have you removed such details? I saw part of them."

I kept silent and did not reply to their shout or threat. I did not even eat their food.

I kept this position a whole day, saying, "Seeing Dad is the price of any information."

They threatened to torture me physically, but I did not surrender. I resisted them for another day. The guard ate pieces of chocolate before me so I would weaken and surrender to them. However, they did not know that my tough conditions made me forget that I was a child enjoying chocolate and toys. They also did not know that I became no longer afraid of threat and shout. I turned into a person I did not know him well. Even if I wanted to surrender, I remembered my father who encouraged me to stay strong before any challenges. His trust in me deprived me of my childhood and raised me to a higher level in life.

I managed to endure the pain of chains as well as hunger and thirst. Finally, their cursed gangster came in the morning of the third day, and said, "What do you want in return for giving us the missing part of the research?"

I smiled confidently, "I want to see my dad."

He pointed to the guard, "Bring her dad!"

I smiled broadly, got up and arranged my hair in preparation for meeting my lovely father. I noticed that the guard's face was changed as if he did not want to implement the order. However, I did not care as I was sure that he would carry out the order forcefully. I just wanted to see my father and hug him. I kept imagining how to meet him some days ago. I imagined that I would see him chained. However, this did not prevent me from feeling happy about meeting him.

The guard came with two men pulling a bed. I said, "It seems that he was tortured; that is why they brought him on a bed." However, I saw him fully covered with a comforter.

I looked with a surprise at the gangster who pointed to the guard, saying, "Unlock the chain!"

He untied my hands and legs, but I was still sitting on the bed. I looked at him brokenheartedly, and said, "I want my dad."

He smiled like a devil, and said, "Will you see Dad this way?"

I moved slowly towards the bed and removed the comforter with my trembling hands to see what I never imagined. I saw my father sleeping peacefully. I shouted painfully and could not control my tears. I was astonished and did not know what to do. I kept kissing his head and hugging him strongly. It seemed that my father was tortured severely before dying as shown from the blue bruises on his face and fingers.

I sat on my knees, and then stood up. I did that several times. I looked at this devil who was looking at me coolly, and the guard who tried to hide his tears from me.

I sighed strongly, shouting, "Dad!" The guard kept me away from the corpse, but the gangster ordered him to leave me.

I stared at the face of my father to make sure that he was already my father. I talked with him so he might reply to me, "Dad, please answer me. Don't keep silent as Mum. They killed Mum before feeding my sister and killed her innocent midwife. Dad, I tried my best to see you but did not wish to see you dead. I don't think that they tortured or even killed you. Dad, I tried to achieve your hope, but you died before feeling proud of me. I became the hero of your story as you were a hero of my stories. Dad, your little daughter will be your next hero. Sleep peacefully!!!"

I was sighing silently and suffering a severe pain to the extent that I could not cry loud. I felt that my heart was pulsing slowly. The gangster caught my forearm and said, "Here you are Dad! Where is the missing part of the research? Where is the tattoo that was drawn on your back?"

While I was sticking to my father's body, the gangster held one of my hands. The other hand was pulling my father's clothes. I said, "The tattoo was transferred to my sister's back."

He shouted, "Which sister?"

I looked at him with anger, confidence and challenge, saying, "My little sister who was with me at the lake."

"Is she the infant who disappeared with the mythical bird?" he asked madly.

He left my hand and kept moving in the room like an angry lion. He abused me, approached from my face and moved away as if he was a ghost. I started to go unconscious, but when I was about to fall on the ground, he hit my shoulders in order to make me regain consciousness. "How can I get your sister? How can I get her back?" he asked.

I did not know how to tell him that if it was possible to get her back, I would not have left her for the bird. I thanked the monsters a lot for helping me although I had nothing to do with them except that we wanted to live peacefully. He disturbed me with his shout. However, I smiled, so he went crazy. His voice faded away, but my father and mother's voices were clearer than the voice of that crazy man. I closed my eyes in order to go away from this place. "Dad, Mum! Where are you?"

I held my father's hand firmly and kept hugging him strongly. Finally, I felt relaxed.

*We think that stories end with sunset, and do not know that another story starts in the next day. There is a giant bird flying in the sky and carrying a little girl on its back. She is wearing a chain around her neck and the tattoo on her back is clearly visible*

# Story 2
# Where Am I?

# "If You Don't Add Something to Life, You Are Nothing." Mostafa Saadeq Al-Rafe'ie

**8 March**
**UK**
**121 Mount St, Mayfair**
**London w2k**
**12:30 p.m.**

In a small apartment on the second floor, the mother opened her wide beautiful eyes after deep sleep. She smiled warmly while reading the congratulation message she received on her mobile phone on the occasion of her thirtieth birthday. At this time, a little black girl with curly hair broke into the mother's room. The seven-year-old girl was wearing a pink pyjama.

The girl raised something she was holding in her hands, and said, "Mum! What is this?"

The mother moved her head to see what the girl was holding in her hands while relaxing on her bed, and said, "What?"

When the mother saw what the girl was holding in her hands, she got up fast while feeling happy and surprised, and then asked her girl, "Lolo, my princess! How have you got it?"

Both the mother and the girl sat down on the floor of the room, and the mother was wearing a black pyjama as if she was in mourning. The girl told her mother that she found it in the black box placed in the closet of obsolete stuff. The object that led to the surprise of the mother and question of the girl was a one-eyed telescope to see the stars.

The mother looked as if she was holding a piece of jewellery, and said, "My princess! This was the telescope of my dad, and then he offered it to me as a present. I used this instrument when I was playing with my friends…I used to look through the telescope and then predict their future. We were young and full of hope and optimism."

"Can we play with it now?" the girl asked innocently.

The mother laughed as if she longed for childhood madness. She stood up, held the hands of her girl and approached the open window. Then, she looked through the telescope, and said to her babe, "My princess, I see you succeeding in your study, being able to achieve your dreams and overcoming your tough circumstances."

The girl held the hand of her mother, and asked her to get down, saying, "What about my nation? Will I see it?"

The mother kept silent, and with two eyes full of tears, she hugged her little girl and said, "You are the nation, my princess."

****

In a very cold dark lab, where you can hear nothing except for the hum of the machines, the computers related to human capsules to follow the vital functions of the bodies in them for years, the signals rose suddenly without any warning and a device flashed out. One of them shouted, "Sir! Someone woke up."

In a state of extreme alert, the medical staff carefully entered the lab and identified the place of the signal. Then, they calmly withdrew the snow liquid and opened the box after raising the temperature to get out the girl from whom the awakening signal was issued.

They put the girl on a moving bed and rushed to one of the nearby warm and safe rooms. Her eyes were rotating between dream and reality and between perception of the moment and retrieval of the past.

The black girl looked as if she was living at the prairie; she was bony and had wide eyes and short hair. She was left on the bed alone after having made sure of her functional safety. The girl was wearing white clothes with short sleeves extending to her knees. She was also wearing a plastic parcel around her left wrist on which a seven-digit number was written.

After a long time, she asked the 170-cm tall military fellow, "Where am I? What is this place?"

The girl kept asking and the military fellow kept staring at her. She realised that he does not understand her, so she tried to speak with him in English, but he kept gazing at her.

After three hours of raising her questions, the girl was taken by a medical staff to one of the upper floors and asked to walk. She went out with them, walking slowly, and was surprised by her inability to walk normally. She entered a large meeting room accommodating more than one hundred persons.

Three persons – two men and a 50-year-old woman – entered this room. The woman welcomed the girl warmly, but she did not care for such kindness and asked her a lot of questions about the place and her conditions.

The woman smiled calmly and asked her to relax, but the girl refused and expressed her willingness to learn everything. When the women saw her insistence, she asked the military fellow, who was carrying a device with his hands, to display the video stored in the digital storage unit. He displayed the three-dimension documentary video which was broadcasted from the middle of the meeting table.

The video displayed a small country known as the "Peace Pigeon". A brutal hand shot this pigeon on one of her wings, then the royal decrees were issued to deport all young people to secret places.

The girl went with her chair backward, unbelieving what the video displayed. The woman understood the girl's conditions and asked to stop the video. Then she started asking the girl, "Please forget what you watched and answer my questions! Could you please talk with me about yourself?"

The girl smiled and said with full confidence, "My name is Nawar, a fresh graduate looking for a suitable job. I am engaged to my colleague and I am preparing for my wedding party."

"When is the wedding party?" the woman asked.

Nawar said, "In mid-August 2018."

The woman exchanged looks with the girl's fellows. The blonde man, who was silent from the beginning, said, "Sorry to tell you that we are in March 2025."

Nobody liked to hear what was said, but Nawar showed her willingness to hear the truth from the beginning. The woman said, "You and the other young people were expelled from your country to live here in Bristol as per the royal decrees."

Nawar's eyes were full of tears and she cried silently. The woman turned her face towards the doors, intending to leave, but Nawar held her hand and asked her insanely, "Why? What is the reason?"

She answered while taking her hands away from Nawar mercilessly without looking at her. She said, "Sorry, I am not authorised to talk about anything."

Nawar burst into tears and was about to have nervous breakdown. The doctor – the blond man – tried to inject her with a sedative but she resisted and refused until she opened her eyes.

Nawar looked at the place, saying, "It is an aeroplane and everyone is in deep sleep." She smiled broadly and saw that she was wearing a light-pink sport suit and not that white dress.

The girl tried to turn on the screen to see the clock after taking a deep breath to relax her nerves after the nightmare she saw. She stood up as if a scorpion bit her and started to remember what happened. It was 2:00 a.m. (30 March 2025) so what she saw was not a nightmare. All people on the board of the plane wear the same dress; sport suits in different colours.

"Are you Nawar?"

The girl moved her face towards the voice to see a short white man and corrective glasses. He was sitting two seats away.

"Thank God for your safety! You slept for a long time because of the injection you took after having a nervous breakdown," the man said.

She widened her eyes and remembered that she was injected despite her refusal and resistance.

"Your mental condition was very bad so I preferred that you sleep for a long time until the plane departs," the man said.

Nawar wiped her forehead with her hands and gathered her strength. The young man felt that Nawar was not OK. He smiled and said, "My name is Omar."

The girl understood that he wanted to change the topic, so she exchanged smile and asked, "Did not anyone tell you more details about our situation?"

Omar shook his head, answering in negative. He leant his seat back to sleep, and said, "Do not worry! We will know the truth soon."

Then he closed his eyes as he was in need of this relaxation.

Nawar relaxed and felt safer after talking with Omar.

The plane landed safely, and unlike any other time, no one rushed to go off. Taking a decision to face the truth is not easy, but in the end, you have to walk through the way chosen by rulers for you.

Thousands of young men got off the plane calmly and silently after thirty-five minutes of landing. However, the airway did not take them to the centre of the airport as usual; it led them to a dark tunnel and a vestibule under the airport.

A young man whispered, "I did not know that there is a big tunnel under our international airport."

"Is there anyone here? Can anyone help us?" one of them said.

"Welcome to the new hope."

Everyone ran towards the voice coming from the dark corners that was lit only by the lighting of computers. Unfortunately, the next voice was coming from a computer. The young men felt disappointed, but the computer did not care and said these words. "Welcome to the new hope, you are in a tunnel connecting the Falk Island to the John Coast under the Gulf water." They went ahead cautiously, and no one knew the enemy.

A 20-year-old girl approached the computer and said, "Why do not you tell us more?"

"Your mother needs you," the computer replied.

Everyone sat down on the floor and the computer repeated its words, "Welcome to the new hope, you are in the tunnel…"

They were stunned to draw any mental image of what could be encountered outside. Some searched the place but did not reach anything.

One of them said, "Our stay here will not change the reality. I think we should go ahead with our journey. The sentence 'your mother needs you' can be a motive to confront the unknown."

"We did not have this tunnel in 2018 so what happened to reach this point," Nawar said while leaning on the concrete wall

A young fatty man with a black thick hair and two small eyes replied, "If the unknown is simple and you want us to face without collecting information about it, the plane would land at our international airport. If the contrary is true."

They became worried again after supporting the words of their friend and did not reach a solution.

Omar tried to convince them to search again for a hidden message they might not have paid any attention to, but their search was just a waste of time and they failed to find anything. They were forced to come out to face the reality.

They proceeded cautiously.

****

**1 April 2025**
**UK**
**Liverpool**
**L69 3BX**
**10:00 a.m.**

The sound of warm applause from one of scientific research halls was aloud. The young man standing behind the podium and wearing a formal suit was full of pride. He was a handsome person, having thick hair and bread. This man looked like the characters of old stories.

The sound of the applause turned down, and everyone awaited the assessment of the committee supervising the research of the students expected to graduate from the faculties of science, engineering and technology to carry out their projects and inventions. Mr Peter, the vice chairman of the Committee, was a 40-year-old paunchy man, wearing a formal suit. He was red-haired and blue-eyed, having bad reputation in devastating the efforts of the Committee. He said with his husky voice after taking the microphone from the young man, "Researcher Omran! You are not really a researcher. I regret to inform you that the Committee apologises for supporting these trivialities. What you submitted is an impossible dream and difficult to be implemented because it will cost us imaginary figures."

The people in the hall objected to this assessment and considered it contrary to the Committee's laws. Omran collected his belongings and shut down the electronic devices, pulling out the digital disks from them. He tried to go out from the hall, but the people asked the Committee to give him another opportunity to present the research to the chairman and the financial officer.

However, Omran refused and accepted his destiny. He was accompanied to the car by Mr Marciz, the supervisor of the research, who was insulting Peter and the other Committee members for not reacting to this wrong decision. He shouted at Omran saying, "Are you okay? How can you refuse another opportunity for presenting your research?"

Omran looked at him bravely, saying, "To increase the value of the research, did you get me?"

While the teacher was talking with his student, his friend Elia, a blonde young man with brown eyes, hurried up to take another appointment for his colleague to present the research. Although the people in the hall were still objecting to the unjustified rejection of the research that may lead to a qualitative leap in the world of technology, Peter had not paid any attention and went to the corner to make a phone call. Elia was curious about hearing the call more than taking an appointment. He approached Peter and heard what he did not like to hear.

Peter flared up and said, "Mrs Rachel! Didn't we agree that such a strange person should not continue making damp inventions? You violated our agreement and both of you and your orphan son will bear the responsibility."

Elia was astonished and tried to concentrate. Peter phoned the dean of Omran's faculty, ordering him to keep away from this issue.

Elia was worried and didn't know what to do. He was surprised at the hatred he saw at Peter's face towards Omran although it was first time to see him. Elia wondered at the agreement that was between Peter and Omran's mother as well as the words "your orphan son".

"Isn't Shaman still alive? Didn't he travel to perform a military duty abroad?" Elia asked himself.

****

**Sea Coast**
**Big Towers**

"Shouldn't we go now? It is the third or fourth day for our stay on the beach," asked one the girls extending her feet to the sea waves.

Another girl answered, "Lets await the group that went to inspect the place."

A young man quickly pointed out to his friends, trying to draw their attention. He was chosen to be the leader of the group. This 30-year-old man had light brown hair, and was characterised by having nasal deviation. He was chosen for his experience in these issues, as he was an active member at the humanitarian and relief campaigns. He asked the group to gather around him to see the plan that all of them should abide with. The young man stood up on a high threshold so that everyone could hear him. He said, "We make an agreement before dispersing."

1- We should be cautious
2- We should not participate in talks with anyone
3- We should control ourselves

"We will be divided into six groups; each group will make sure of the news and then come back after three days."

The young people inhaled the air of the country, and all of them dispersed. It was striking that streets were very calm.

The desired destination was very away. An 18-year-old man said some negative words to his group while moving to street opposite the small park next to the museum. The young man heard the sound of a parked car as if it was ready to move. He moved towards this car and intended to open its door. Nawar reproved and quarrelled with him.

"You aren't responsible for me?" the young man shouted.

Striking his shoulder, Nawar said, "Salman! I am not responsible for you and don't want to be, but there is an agreement with Mohammed, and you must abide by it. We should not play with something if we cannot bear its consequences."

A young bald man in his late twenties, with thick beard intervened, saying, "What's wrong with you?"

Nawar bit Salman's arm for ignoring her and paying attention to the young man, so he kept crying and grew angry. The young man repeated his question with a louder voice, "What's wrong with you?"

Nawar held one of the girls' hands away from her, saying, "He wants to get into a car to reach our destination fast."

They shouted again with a louder voice.

Meshaal stood up and led the group to the small green square that was opposite their destination on the street. It was clear that life was fading from this place as hope was taken from the hearts of several young men.

Salman replied sarcastically, "Do you think you can change this gloom that surrounds us?"

Meshaal smiled and said, "We will not get rid of this gloom and nightmare, but we can sleep to dream."

Calmness prevailed among the young people.

Meshaal asked them to close their eyes, and with the sunset, he narrated the story they knew about themselves with a voice full of love, completed its details with a depressive voice and ended it with a voice full of hope to face the unknown whatsoever.

Meshaal had the ability to change the tone of his voice and feeling from pain to hope. The young people opened their eyes and said, "We did not want to return to our reality."

He smiled at them calmly and stood up to shake the dust from his hands and cloth, saying, "Stop praising me! Let's listen to every one of you!"

Meshaal was not a leader and did not fight to be, but there are simple things that make some people look like as leaders. With his sincere desire, Meshaal tried to calm down the young people whose talk was full of ambition. They started to talk about their skills and all of them were awaiting their turns with ambition.

They turned their hearts around each other in warmth to listen to the poem of their colleague Yusuf. He was a black man, having curly hair.

They filled these hours with their laugh and voices that embraced the stars. They stripped their thoughts of any concern and plunged into the sea of play. When their spirits flew away from the reality of the moment, they thanked Meshaal for opening the door that they needed. At 8:00 p.m., they completed their journey to achieve their goal with all energy and positivity.

It was the time to have dinner in the light of candles in one of the old English-style restaurants in Liverpool. In 2025, it is rare to find a restaurant where a waiter is a real person. Today, the robots are the ones who do the job.

Elia sat alone on the table in his dark blue shirt, waiting for an important guest, but was surprised to see Omran alone wearing his sportswear. Elia resisted his curiosity at first but surrendered and pointed to his friend to come and share the table. Omran was surprised by the table equipment. He nodded with his eyes, saying, "Romantic appointment."

Elia laughed and said, "I lost my heart a long time ago, what about your heart?"

Omran just smiled, "Let my heart alone! What are doing here alone?"

Elia did not tell the truth and said, "Dr Leva is preparing for travel and I invited her for dinner. What about you?"

"I came to this restaurant to forget my mind, running away from you, but it seems that your destiny wants to disturb you," Omran answered while feeling disappointed.

Elia looked worried and feared that Peter has done what he thought of. Omran quickly confirmed his fear, saying, "I received an e-mail saying that the university decided to send me for an alternative task related to the project that was rejected. I have to complete this job until I graduate."

Eliah's tongue slipped and insulted Peter again, asking him, "Didn't they tell you where they will send you?"

Omran shook his head, "Yes, to the dead country."

Omran then asked, "What is Peter's relationship to sending me abroad?"

However, he could not get an answer because Dr Levia arrived at this moment. Elia stood up and introduced them to each other. Dr Levia smiled and sat down. She looked attractive with her brown hair falling on her shoulders. The yellow dress she was wearing made her look like a sun shining in the dark.

\*\*\*\*

Again, the sun set and moved away from the horizon, leaving the hope of rise in the minds of young people. At this night, the young people arrived at the chosen governorates. Small groups were distributed to make accurate exploration. They had tough conditions, as exploring the unknown is not that easy.

The group of Meshaal arrived at Al-Qurn Museum late at night.

Despite the lapse of several years, this edifice still maintains its importance. Some young people at the age of thirties refrained from entering the museum on the grounds that it was difficult to find something related to their cause. However, they were, in fact, fleeing the pain of remembering their wounds.

A thin girl with delicate features covering her hair with the hat attached to her clothes groped at the walls of the house. She said, "I hear a voice calling from inside."

Salman looked at her derisively, "Please Mariam, time and place are not suitable for your feelings."

"Why?" Mariam wondered innocently although she was older than Salman.

Salman's mood changed suddenly and stopped participating in the conversation. Mariam was determined to know the reason, but he shouted at her, so Meshaal intervened to separate them. Salman asked him about his bad temper. Salman sat on the floor as if he wanted to cry. He said, "I find it hard to accept this situation. I need to cry but I cannot."

Meshaal brought him to his chest as if he were embracing his young son, trying to calm him down and reassure him that things would be okay, god willing.

The girls tried to convince Mariam to remain as silent as possible and stop her urgency as children because this would bring problems. However, she insisted on her stubbornness and put her hands in the pockets of her trousers and walked away from the circle of advice.

At midnight, the helicopters began circling in the sky to undertake a night inspection. The young people rushed inward involuntarily, fearing that this aerial survey would be dangerous for them.

They took advantage of the darkness in the museum and sat under the stairwell as if they were refugees in their homeland. Some of them stared for remembering those bitter days around 35 years ago.

The helicopters kept flying in the sky almost until dawn, and then withdrew calmly.

None of them slept as fear made them stay awake this time.

Nawar was scared and said, "Can I speak now?"

All of them looked at her. She said, "I have lost three young men since yesterday."

Meshaal was shocked and shouted angrily, "Who are they? Why didn't you tell us in the moment?"

She said and tears were about to spill forth, "They are Zamzam, Dana and Faisal."

Before Meshaal shouted at her, Yusuf had whispered in his ear, "Calm down! The girl is afraid and not guilty."

"Why did not you tell us since yesterday?" asked Mashaal while trying to keep calm.

"It was not the right time and the helicopters were moving over our heads," she answered while nodding her head.

Silence prevailed for moments.

Then a young man, called Khaled, offered a new suggestion. This boarded-shouldered man was bald but was not that tall. He said, "Meshaal! Let me and Yusuf go and look for them. You and the other young people should go to explore this place."

Meshaal agreed without thinking and the other two young men went to look for their lost friends.

****

There were almost 700 people in the area looking for any evidence or message left by one of the lost persons. The sun shone to light up the memories. The past has not changed anything, whether smell, effects, or feelings.

"You will not be stopped by anyone," said Hessa, a 28-year-old girl. "In front of this edifice, you must be ashamed."

No one commented on her statement.

The search journey began silently. They searched between the reinforced concrete pillars of the house and the cars parked in front of the house, and in the tiny white microbus tattooed with gunshots. They searched under the picture frames but found nothing.

When they moved to the second museum, they had to pass through corridors and spaces connecting the two houses. The corridors were full of pictures and some old manuscripts. The young people spread in the place to explore and recall memories. A short black girl covering her head with a floral piece of cloth and wearing a loose dress said, while pointing to some of the wall-hung manuscripts, "There's something strange about the paintings."

Someone asked her, "What is there, Elaf?"

"The paragraphs are not ordered and the sentences are not linked. Surely, someone played with them," she answered.

The young people brought the manuscripts and arranged the paragraphs and sentences. After completing the task, they found nothing interesting, except that the manuscript returned as it was. One of them looked behind the papers and found a cartoon drawn with the pencil.

"This is the signature of the cartoonist, and this is also the signature of the painter Ghaith," said Dr Bashayer, a 30-year-old woman who was almost fat.

They all exchanged looks, asking themselves, "What is meant by these drawings? What is the message to be delivered?" Such paintings carry the signatures of famous painters. They had the same drawings, but the signatures below them were different. All of them had a hand tightening its grip on a man and inserting him into the computer screen.

\*\*\*\*

## Great Hospital – Liverpool
## Laboratory Suites

While walking in the corridors of the hospital, Elia was preoccupied with Omran's travel. Suddenly, he found himself before Dr Leva's office. Elia knocked on the door because he found it a good opportunity to talk with her. Leva did not answer him because she was busy with her work. Upon seeing him, she smiled shyly and welcomed him. Leva stopped his contemplation at her angelic countenances, and said, "Welcome, trainee doctor."

He smiled at her, and then she asked him about the important subject that concerned him. Elia got worried and did not know whether it was right to tell her or not. She quickly got worried, so he told her to relieve her concern.

Elia talked with her about Omran's project, the rejection of the assessment committee, Peter's talk with Omran's mother Rachel and the dean's decision.

"If you like your friend, don't tell him now! What you said may be just whims resulting from your concern. Let him travel to achieve his goal and provide us with evidence for what you said! Don't confuse him as he already has enough concerns!" Levia said to him.

Elia asked her curiously, "How can we get evidence?"

She reassured him that she had a way, so Elia breathed a sigh of relief when he knew that he could protect his friend from any harm. He asked to leave to pay farewell to Omran who was travelling on that day.

Elia left the hospital for the train station, from where the train would take his friend to the airport. He went to bid farewell to his friend who accompanied him since the last year of the high school. Elia adored the insane silence of his friend and loved the ambition that is embedded behind his calm.

After arriving at the train station, Elia found that the train moved away and just saw the last locomotive of it.

\*\*\*\*

The moments went on, the stories were written and the tricks were made. The young people were still looking for the means to help them save the nation. Those people chosen to inspect the courtyard and the legal houses came to blows and shouted at each other loudly.

They had conflicted views; some of them refused to enter such places to maintain their moral and material values and confidentiality, while the other people saw that they should have searched all places. They quarrelled with hands.

Zaid shouted at one of the opponents, "Do you think that what you do serves the nation? If you remain stubborn, all of us will sink."

Tying a veil on her head, Noor confirmed his opinion, saying, "We are not violating the sanctity of the place, but we need to find our rescuer."

However, these words did not convince any of the opponents and they kept quarrelling, forcing the other group to sneak into the court for search and inspection. Amid this quarrel, the search was useless because the court was empty of papers, documents and computers, as if someone had done it deliberately. It was a building deprived of all details.

In the opera house, such a piece of art that caused a stir in the first days of its opening, the young people entered the theatre, ignoring all the emotions that could be control them. They started to play on the stage; they sometimes played a scene from the memory on the stage and sometimes sang some songs despite lack of harmony between voices.

As the young people drowned in the atmosphere of entertainment away from their goal, the lights were turned off suddenly. Between scream and escape, the lights were turned on again and many young people were lost in a strange way; they might have been kidnapped. The other young people were astonished, and fear spread in the place, so they went out of the place as if they were captives. They kept running until they reached the flag field beside the big fountain. Suddenly, the fountain started the automatic show accompanied by some national songs as usual, so the young people burst into tears.

A voice was heard warning them, "Be careful! The enemy is watching over you. What you are looking for is with the mother and her daughter. Hurry up! We are captives without restrictions or walls. We are captives in an unknown world."

A young girl went to her colleague, who were terrified and held her hand, saying, "Is not that the voice of the artist Subhi?"

A white tall slim man shouted, "This is the voice of my father."

One of his friends held his hand. "Jassim, Calm down!"

However, he pulled the collar of his friend and shouted, "Abdullah, have you heard what my father said, 'they are captives'."

Abdullah put his hands on the face of his friend and addressed him harshly while looking at his eyes, saying, "He said that they were captives, which means that he was not alone. Calm down to know what we can do."

Jassim calmed down, but his eyes were full of tears.

The other people kept pursuing their goal. One of them came to the office of the inventor 'Sadiq Qassem' at the Centre for Talent and Creativity, believing that such a character should leave behind a message.

"Friends, we have to search in a different way," said a white girl with long black hair.

Omar asked her, "What do you mean, Bibi?"

"Of course, a person like Sadiq Qassem would not leave a message in a clear way. The message would be revealed only by those who are looking for it," she answered.

They nodded their heads in acceptance of Bibi's idea.

They searched the office, the computer, the shelves and the books, but did not see the message that was right before their eyes. Badr, a 20-year-old white man with soft hair and light grey stomach, put his hand on the desk, and said, "Will we come back disappointed?"

No one commented on Badr's question, but at the same moment his voice was full of hope. "Could we find the message?" he asked.

They put what was in their hands and looked at Badr. He quickly removed the objects from the desk and ran his hands over it. Badr found words engraved in the form of symbols in a very precise way that no one could pay attention to.

※※※※

After several days from the agreed time, the young people met on the seashore next to the towers as agreed so each group can unveil the results it reached. Unfortunately, several persons were controlled by despair and surrender, and preferred to leave the country and return to the UK.

Mohammed climbed the concrete barrier and asked all of his colleagues to sit down, saying, "We have important information we should benefit from;

- Al-Qurn Museum has night guards
- Five young people were lost in such area
- There are two dead persons in the port
- The drawings indicate the computers have a secret
- All computers have been tampered with in their mother tongue
- There is a voice message from the artist Subhi
- There is a written message from the inventor Sadiq Qassem
- We lost a large number of young people at the Opera House

"This is evidence that we do not live alone on the earth, and the enemy is very near to us."

A short black young man with two adjacent eyebrows said angrily, "I don't like your way of working."

He then went away from the place.

Abdul Aziz shouted at him and said, "Suhaib, the land is not secure."

Suhaib didn't reply and went away. Mohammed then tried to calm them down, and said, "Anger and despair make him hear himself only. We should have housing near the seashore to gather in one place."

They chose a hotel that was located near the seashore, and all of them agreed on this choice.

Nobody knew when he would avoid the foolishness he possessed. Suhaib was walking aimlessly in the streets of the country. Suddenly, he stumbled to the foot of one of them, and stood up feeling the panic of his fall.

A voice of apology was heard, "If I know that there are others living on this land, I will not sit in the middle of the road."

Suhaib replied, "If I know that there are other people here, I will not walk on this street."

The strange person extended his hand to shake hand, and said, "My name is Omran."

However, Suhaib turned his back, "I do not care."

Before going away, Omran asked him, "Are there other people on this land?"

"There are several people on the seashore," Suhaib replied without looking at him.

He then continued his journey to the unknown.

In the house, embracing the kind mother and her innocent daughter, the mother felt afraid since her daughter said, "Mother, you are the nation." She kept roaming at the room while wearing short, long-sleeved black dress and having her hair raised like a lioness in a cage. The mother predicted the occurrence of a danger after an old woman tried to bait Lolo and enforced her to get into a car while she was getting out of her school. Unless the guards intervened, the little girl would be lost.

The daughter kept thinking until the sun rise of the third day and prevented her daughter from going to the school. She made a call and tried to reassure herself, saying, "There is a solution…Of course, I will find a solution."

The phone kept ringing for long, and then the other party replied, "Welcome Atyab!"

She swallowed her saliva and approached the phone more from her ear, saying, "Do you remember when I came here seven years ago, running away from everything and carrying only my official papers and my three-month-old daughter?"

"I remember that well," he answered with amazement.

The mother looked like as if she wanted to cry, and said, "After securing housing for us, you told me that you could provide us with a safer place when I need it."

"Did you face something wrong?" he replied with concern.

The mother burst into tears and said: "Eugene! Please take me to the farthest point from here; my daughter is in danger."

He tried to calm her down, but she insisted: "Believe me, I don't have time. They reached my daughter at the school, and I expect them to break into my house at any moment."

He said reassuringly: "Listen to me well, the danger toddling around you and your daughter may be different from the danger you think of. However, I will send you a team in two or three hours to help you come to me. I have moved to Liverpool three months ago."

She answered him without thinking: "I will collect my stuff and get ready to go out."

She hanged up the phone and started to collect her stuff madly. The little girl, who was standing on the threshold, didn't understand anything and was worried about her mother. Thirty minutes after Eugene's call, she received another call from the police station, asking her to come immediately. She tried to call Eugene to tell him, but all phone numbers were busy. Thus, she gave in to the emergency and took her daughter and went to the police station, without changing her black dress or even combing her hair.

The officer said that the school had told them about an attempt to kidnap a girl, so they arrested the woman who tried to commit such a crime. Atyab sighed and sat down on the chair, asking to have a glass of water.

They brought her a glass of water and the officer ordered the woman to come in. A young white woman with short curly hair came in. "My mother, this is the woman who tried to get me into the car," said Lulu.

The officer asked her: "Lulu, do you know her?"

She nodded without saying a single word.

He said to her, "But the woman who tried to bait you was old and had white hair."

The girl looked at him and her eyes were filled with fear. "I know her from the burning sign at her hand, because she gave me the candy with the same hand, and I asked her about the burning."

Then he ordered the officer to take her out of the room. "I do not understand anything," Atyab said.

He told her that the investigations indicated that this woman was a member of the child trafficking gang and wanted to kidnap the little girl because she had no data or a homeland that would demand her rights if she was kidnapped.

Atyab hugged her daughter and burst into tears out of the severe psychological pressure she had.

\*\*\*\*

Stranger reached the seashore, where the young people were sitting. His arrival caused a state of confusion and tension among the young people. He does not share something with them except the black colour of hair.

"I thought that I live alone on this land," said Omran while trying to start talking with the young people.

When none reacted to him, he said, "I didn't intend to intrude upon you, but I am a stranger on this land."

Mohammed replied, "We have just arrived at this land, welcome!"

Omran thought that they were students who came to carry out some projects and didn't think that they were the owners of the land. However, the young people believed that the stranger was a spy and claimed innocence. Each party retained his thought for itself.

In the evening, they kept mediating at the stars whose light reflected on the sea, and they sat waiting for the other colleagues to tell them how to carry out the next step. They were sure that the calmness carries a lot of secrets and surprises.

Omran approached two men whispering away from the beach and leaning on the towers there. He said, "May I interrupt your talk?"

The short girl with curly hair smiled and said, "Welcome!"

However, Badr turned his face away, so Omran apologised again.

Badr shouted, "Don't apologise, you interrupted our talk."

The girl tried to calm him down, but he rebuked her in English so Omran could understand. "Didn't you meet him with smile? Joori, continue then talking with him."

Badr turned his back to them and moved away. Omran tried to stop him but he was very angry and did not respond. Omran apologised for the third time, asking, "I don't know why you are so cautious about dealing with me. Aren't we all here to pursue one goal and carry out the graduation project?"

Joori was surprised and asked, "Which graduation?"

He looked at her in astonishment and said, "Aren't you students at the University of Liverpool?"

She shook her head. "Omran, we are here to restore life to this land; you stand on our homeland."

The girl told him their story in full, from the minute of their wake-up in Bristol to that moment. She also told him why Badr lost his temper. "He tried to explore the internet for any news or events telling us about the past seven years, but he did not find any information as if someone was deliberately hiding the facts."

While the picture became clear to Omran, it remained almost unclear for Jassim and Abdullah.

They went out of the park, which was located on Soor Street, with the insistence of Abdullah to change the mood of his friend after what happened at the opera house. Upon leaving the park, they met Suhaib who was tampering with a car. He changed his clothes and wore the *dishdasha* and it seemed that he stayed some days at his home.

The two men tried to convince him to go back with them and stop tampering with the unknown, but he refused as if he was a small child and kept trying to turn on the car.

Upon turning on the car, the sound of the engine grew louder, and Suhaib disappear with a car. Jassim and Abdullah shouted madly and moved back and forth in the place, but they found no trace. They returned like crazy to the beach, shouting loudly, asking for help from everyone.

After thirty minutes of running, they stood among the young people, feeling exhausted and tired and causing stress to all people. They grew terrified after hearing the incident of Suhaib.

Nawar shouted at Salman, "Did you know why I quarrelled with you when you wanted to tamper with the car?"

Mohammed felt nervous and didn't know how to handle the issue. He only asked the young people to decipher the message which the inventor Sadiq Qassem left behind.

It was really midnight that day when the young people finished deciphering the message from symbols engraved on the wooden desk, which they took with them, to a message written on the paper. They then read the message in public.

"Our dear young men, male and female, at the time you read the message, know that we are in a prison with no doors and under a psychologically painful restraint torturing us. We don't have time to fight or confront because our enemy is invisible.

"Now the field is for you, beware of the electronic stuff and the indoor whether buildings or boxes. Choose always the outdoor, read the 'wonders of inventions' book and follow the steps."

Bibi delivered the book to Mohammed after finding it in the boxes that were taken from the inventor's office to the beach.

However, the pages of the book were burnt.

They were amazed at how to get information from the black pages. Omran crossed through the young people and said to Mohammed, "Can I have a look at the book?"

Zaid hurried up and said, "Thanks, this is none of your business."

However, Omran completed his talk with Mohammed, saying, "But I am specialised in scientific inventions."

Mohammed gave him the book, hoping to get a result. He turned the pages and said, "I will decipher the symbols and you carry out the steps, and then give me what I want to go back to my homeland."

Mohammad shook hands with Omran and agreed with his opinion.

From the moment of declaring the agreement between the young people and Omran, the issues were settled between the two parties. However, there was still something between Leva and Elia in Liverpool, especially after Elia had told Omran the information they received. While moving on Mount James Street near Liverpool Cathedral at a calm night, Leva stopped and looked at her friend. He asked her, "What's wrong?"

"When will you tell Omran the information you have?" she asked while being kindled with anger.

He turned away his face, saying, "Leva, it is cold and you're sick. We'll be late for the dinner."

"I don't know which heart you carry between your ribs, how can you keep silent about such dangerous information?" she said with indignation.

He shouted, "Rest assured, I don't have a heart after the information I got. I can't tell him 'my friend, your life is a lie and your presence where you are is the reality'."

However, Leva wasn't affected by his loud voice, and shouted back at him, "I will call him if you won't."

He was agitated like boiling water and got out his phone to call Omran.

The phone kept ringing for long and Elia was about to end the call, but his sleepy friend answered the call. They exchanged greetings and Omran told him that he was about to go back to his homeland. He didn't give Elia a chance to talk as he kept expressing his longing. Elia couldn't react to him well, which surprised Omran and let him ask about the reason.

"Listen, I need you to do something for me," Elia said.

Omran got up from his bed in the hotel, asking, "What's wrong?"

Elia said, "I will send you a digital address with certain coordinates of where you are, please go there and look at the details."

Although Omran was surprised by his friend's request, he promised to do so as soon as possible.

Elia ended the call and looked at Leva's face angrily. "Can we go now?"

He silently walked ahead of him.

In the morning that was scheduled for meeting Omran to start implementing the agreement, all people were surprised by the absence of the strange young man who agreed to help them in return for taking what he wanted and leaving safely. They all had doubts about his absence, but none knew that Omran didn't come because he became aware of the fake reality.

At this moment, Omran arrived at the destination and stood with a surprise in front of a large quiet house. He hesitated to enter as the place was very rough. However, Omran overcame such feelings and entered without resistance to fulfil his promise.

He stopped in the middle of the house and noticed strange smell, as if he knew it. He inspected all rooms, neglecting the strange smell he experienced. However, his inspection came with no results. He asked, "What does Elia want from this house?"

He noticed a door having a fingerprint scanner in the middle and closed with a password. He then surrendered and turned his back, but his phone rang which stopped him at the ladder.

"Hello Mum, miss you so much, I thought you forgot me."

"My son, where are you? How are you?" his mother asked him yearningly.

He said, "I will come back soon; I have a mission to finish."

She asked him, "What are you doing now?"

"Elia asked me to discover one of the deserted houses," he replied.

Omran noted that his mother's voice changed after the final sentence. She said, "Which discovery? You have to finish the graduation project and return to Liverpool immediately."

While talking to his mother, Omran received a text message from Elia, asking him, "What happened?"

Omran got confused and ended the call with his mother. He then told Elia that he failed to fulfil the mission as the door had a fingerprint scanner. Without thinking, Elia said, "Go back and open the door with your fingerprint."

"Elia, are you aware of what you're saying?" Omran asked.

Elia replied, "I have never been conscious like this before."

Omran disregarded his mother's advice and returned to test the fingerprint while feeling sure that what Elia asked was nonsense. Elia didn't end the call with Omran to make sure that the latter entered the room. However, Omran was completely surprised when the door opened with his fingerprint. He waited for seconds before pushing the door with his fingertips. The secret room extended its arms and embraced him with longing. He moved forward motivated by Elia who was still on the line. Omran moved forward and the past woke up with the bitter reality.

Omran looked attentively at the walls and the pictures hanging on them. He took a deep breath while reading the English manuscripts, dated almost seven or eight years ago.

He shed tears and went out of the house, leaving all the doors open. After an hour of crying like a little child who lost his parents in the crowd, he breathed a sigh of relief, returned to the room and took all the disks, gold electronic chips and the memory notebook.

Omran was then disturbed by the phone ringing and answered the call in a strange voice, saying, "Listen Elia, I am sure you know where you sent me, but I am Omran, son of Shaman, the British young man, don't like to talk about the incredible stuff I saw inside."

"But Peter won't leave you alone. I fear that he may kill you as he did your father," Elia replied with concern.

Omran reproved him, saying: "Elia, may father Shaman was a commander in the Navy Forces and I won't accept belonging to this place. As for Peter, I have what makes him turn away from hurting me and my mother Rahel. This vulgar man is not of British race; I am the strongest party."

Omran ended the call without saying bye to his friend. He became a person other than the one who left the house in the morning and returned to the beach to find all of them waiting for him. They kept looking at him with hope and fear, but he paid no attention. He kept collecting some things he had left on the beach in the evening and moved away riding a motorcycle.

Mutlaq asked him, "Where are you going?"

Manal also asked, "Where is your promise of helping us?"

Feeling irritated, Omran said, "Leave me, it is your problem, not mine. Why should I help you?"

Manal asked him calmly, "Because you also need something. In return for helping us, you will get what ensures your graduation."

Omran answered with pride, "I am the owner of inventions and creative thoughts. I don't need anything from you. Who are you to be in your teams?"

"We are those whose fathers were concerned about and hid us in order to keep us safe. We are those who were trusted by the government officials, and we are those who were sent to another country to get saved. We are those who face the bitter reality," Nawar said angrily.

The young people intervened to calm her down and keep her away in order to not beat Omran. He also moved away and then cried crazily, "I am not from among you." He then moved away quickly, surprising all of them by his strange behaviour.

Fatima, a 22-year-old tall girl, said, "He will come back…Such people cannot tolerate the hardship of the road."

All of them supported their friends' opinion and decided to carry out the mission of deciphering the secret of pages themselves. They began to write down the names of scientific specialists to evaluate the work, and they thought that they were able to perform the mission.

****

One evening, the five missing youths arrived a while ago Khalid, Youssef, Faisal, Dana and Zamzam to tell them with all tiredness that children and the elderly are in shelters down the big island. Muhammad asked how they were doing. Khalid smiled and said that the one who lives on hope, there is no fear for him.

"How can someone with broken heart live? Will our concern protect him?"

After leaving the young people, Omran got lost in the country and kept disregarding the calls of his friend. He then went to Al Sami Cultural Centre that is considered a masterpiece. He sat and kept thinking. Finally, he phoned the dean of his faculty to take the phone number of Mr Peter.

Omran was very tough in the call, and this confused the dean who responded to Omran's request lest the latter should have unveiled his plan.

Feeling extremely tired, Omran phoned Peter.

The latter answered with his husky voice, "Who are you?"

"I am Omran, whom you destroyed," Omran replied while feeling disappointed.

Peter laughed provocatively and asked, "Are you still alive?"

Omran controlled his temper and said, "I want to make a deal."

Peter kept listening to Omran who said with a rough voice, "I want to go back to Liverpool in return for the golden cells I took from Dr Salem's office. I want to graduate from the university in return for giving up my dream."

"Why?" Peter asked.

Omran said, "I don't want to reveal the secret of my belonging to this place."

Peter laughed and said, "Who advised you to do so?"

Omran kept silent for a while and said, "Elia asked me to inspect a house and I discovered this reality. I don't feel or remember my belonging to this place. I don't care about the information he got. I just need to go back to my previous life."

Peter kept silent for long and said, "Well, I need the blue cells and not the golden ones, whatever the cost, and I promise you a better life."

Omran told him that he had met the young people and they were seeking to bring life back to this land regardless of the cost and they found a book of an inventor including solutions for their problems.

He said to Omran, "Listen, we have to find the blue cells. Watch them and tell me their steps and I promise you a better life."

It was funny to promise him a better life as if he was unaware of the reality that the man can never return to his better life after facing bitter experiences or adventures. Of course, Omran's desire to return to the embrace of his mother made him hurry to implement what this evil pirate asked without thinking.

He kept silent for a while and then they asked him, "Why have you returned to us?"

"I apologise. I sat alone with myself and considered all issues," Omran said.

All of them rejected his apology except for Mohammed and Khalid. Nour said, "The land was stolen from us because we are very good."

"And God will return it to us because we are very good," Meshaal said.

****

**UK**
**127 Dale St, Liverpool**
**L2 2JH**
**National Museums Liverpool**

At the National Museums Liverpool, Atyab was talking with Eugene, a 40-year-old man, with an athletic body and grey hair, while walking behind Lulu who was contemplating the exhibits with passion and excitement.

He said, "You are safe now; I repeat it for you."

Feeling worried, she asked, "What do you know about my story?"

He looked at her and said, "Political refugee!"

"How can I be like this and you received a request from my country to protect me and my country?" she laughed involuntarily.

He couldn't answer her, so she said, "I am worried about my daughter, not myself, and I came as a refugee not to protect me but to protect my homeland."

"I don't understand anything, but I will protect you," he said.

They kept silent and monitored Lulu who was happy with this visit.

****

**Big Towers**

Events stop suddenly, allowing us to take a breath.

In this quiet evening, some of the young people were relaxing on the sand of the beach, while others were running in the fresh air.

Manal and Maram – a white girl with brown hair and soft hair – were sitting on the beach while leaning on each other and playing with the sand.

Maram asked, "Manal, are you confident in your sense?"

"Of course, I even feed and train it in order not to make a mistake," Manal said while smiling.

Maram asked, "What does your sense tell you about such conditions?"

Looking at the sky, Manal said, "Don't worry, everything will be okay."

"But I don't like this crisis to end," Maram said.

Manal sat in front of Maram and said, "Why? What is the reason?"

With eyes full of hope, Maram said, "Look at our unity and cooperation; we can't lose this feeling for a moment. What is funny is that we can't move away from the beach in order not to be alone. We work without having Oedipus complex."

"What is our complex?" Manal laughed and asked.

Maram answered seriously, "Our complex is the origin, doctrine, orientation, racism and selfishness."

Manal laughed aloud and said, "We are in 2025 and still have this way of thinking."

Relaxing on the sand and looking at the stars, Maram said, "You will see. Once things are back to where they were, everything will be the same."

Manal got up and gave hand to help her up. "Don't be pessimistic, let's run with our friends."

Every one of us tries to achieve his dreams as much as he can. However, if a blow comes from behind to scatter his dreams and wishes, he will be agitated like boiling water and burn everyone around him. The brave person is the one who can overcome such conditions.

However, it seems that Omran couldn't overcome the reality he saw at such a house because he was still answering the calls of his friend Elia who was extremely worried about him. At this late time, he phoned Omran's mother to ask her about him, but she didn't answer the calls. She was not at her home for the third day in a row.

He closed the door of his house firmly out of anger.

"What's wrong?" Eugene asked.

Elia turned to him in horror, "Brother, when did you come?"

Eugene shut the book and said, "I was off today so I came early. What's wrong with you?"

"My idiot friend Omran doesn't answer my calls and Mrs Rachel was lost a week ago," Elia said.

Eugene, Elia's eldest son, didn't comment and resumed reading the book calmly, showing that the issue didn't deserve his anger. Elia didn't also know that Omran didn't answer his mother's calls and that he was under Peter's control.

\*\*\*\*

**From Dream to Reality**

After almost one and a half months, the young people had found the right way.

On Wednesday, 3:00 p.m., the cries of the victory awaiting the homeland were heard from the beach, almost two kilometres away from the towers. They were dancing and hugging before the circular system connected to the computer screens.

Salman cried, "O crazy, I love you all."

Mohammed smiled and said, "If the land speaks, it will tell you that it is proud of you."

Jassim said, "I am very excited about what this device will offer us. The inventor Sadiq Qassem leaves valuable things."

All of them stood with enthusiasm, love and warmth around the device, which is a circle of computer screens connected to each other. They were connected to digital panels in the centre, working with solar energy through black panels installed as a base having some laser cells which the inventor Sadiq referred to in his letter.

After turning on all screens at the same time, they issued orders to the digital panels with a disturbing loud sound that was about to hurt their hearing. The sound was lowered gradually, and light was emitted from the central point showing a picture below which there was a fifteen-second counter.

The picture was for the inventor Sadiq Qassem, and the young people tried to communicate with him, but it was clear that this was a pre-recorded message and not a direct communication with him. The young people exerted efforts to open the box of the recorded messages. The inventor said: "Your arrival to this point and hearing my message mean that you are fine, I am proud of you I collected some messages I hope to benefit you in your work."

The picture was then faded amid the silence of young people.

Mohammed asked the young people to restart the system, for their appearance Dr Salem's image, Imran's heart jumped out of place, and call to hear his heartbeat, the picture that is in the picture. "Are you willingly looking for a daughter in London?"

Restarting the screens, the picture of the inventor Dr Ahmed Nabil was displayed, to say, "Coffee, sleep, fatigue, race against time, stress, and sometimes frustration, or attempt to give up, but I have a strong belief that you will complete it because you are a fighter and know that the end deserves these efforts."

The picture faded away.

Mohammed restarted the screens madly, which made him lose his temper after being a good example of quiet and patience. Some young men tried to calm him down. Mashaal asked him, "What's wrong with you? Calm down please!"

He sat down on the ground, leaning his head on hands and putting it on his legs. "We exerted more efforts and achieved this great success thanks to love strength and Allah's help. He asks us to look for a mother and her daughter in London!!! Doesn't he know that London is very big?"

Mutlaq said, "Don't worry, Omran will help us."

Omran looked with astonishment. "What can I offer?"

"You can communicate with the concerned authorities in London to help us in the search process, as they are aware of our story because we have been before in Bristol," Khalifa said.

Feeling disappointed, Yusuf said, "Who doesn't know the story of the homeland whose people were dislodged without a war?"

Omran smiled and said, "I will do my best."

Some young people kept thinking of the recorded messages, while Omar was discussing the messages he heard with Othman, an ambitious black thin man.

Omran said, "I think these messages are the keys of the closed boxes."

Othman said, "They are just tips and we have to go back to them when necessary. We don't know what we will face."

The talk between them was about to turn into a fight but Faisal and Abdullah intervened to calm them down. A state of anxiety prevailed among the young people, and it was difficult to find a calm person who can think well.

\*\*\*\*

When the destiny decides something, we should either give up or object to getting out of the way. We are as we want to be.

Rachel sat in front of Peter in his huge, upscale office, where millions of digital coins were placed to show this rare sight.

She sat before him with her pale, sick face begging him. "Please Peter, don't hurt my son, do whatever you want with me, but send a plane to bring him back from this land."

He laughed and said, "Your son who is not answering your calls! Listen, don't worry, he will come back."

She breathed with satisfaction, but he completed. "This will happen if he finishes his mission; otherwise he would remain where the state was in 2018."

Before commenting, he added: "If you incite or call him to disobey my orders, I will tell him who killed his father and who took him to the psychiatrist to erase his memory in order to care for the lovely child."

She swallowed her saliva and kept silent out of fear. He said, "Your son knows that he belongs to that land but watch out for your actions with me in order to not to unveil the other issues."

She kept silent and withdrew silently. After leaving, Peter's phone rang, and he smiled saying, "Welcome, you are my eyes that watch without betraying."

Then he began to listen carefully, and his countenances changed to seriousness. Then he asked, "Are you sure? Well, I'll send you a phone number of someone in London and I trust him very much, he'll definitely help you."

"You waited seven years and now you are about to reap fruit," he said.

As the pace of events accelerated, the young people were waiting for Omran's contact with the person in-charge in London to know the results of his search for the mother and her daughter.

After they decided to meet in the evening because of the high temperature, the young people went out as agreed upon from the hotel International Hotel on 34Street, heading to the beach beside the towers.

Omran received a call at the right time, but he didn't want for the first time to answer it. He was upset because the young people treated him well and he tried to betray them.

Noor asked, "Won't you answer?"

"Yes, now," he said while thinking incoherently.

He answered the phone and the caller said, "I'm glad to tell you that I found the required information. A refugee came in mid-2018 with an official letter from her country. Her name is Taybah and was changed to Atyab. I have recently moved from London to Liverpool with one of our employees, Eugene. I will send you a text message whose old address is in London and you may need it. I will send you Eugene's address in Liverpool."

Omran replied calmly: "Thank you."

Breathing a sigh of relief, Omran ended the call and steered at the young people, saying, "We have to travel now to London."

They exchanged looks and Mohammed said, "It is enough to be accompanied by Meshaal, Khalifa and Bibi."

He shook his head in approval and said, "We should move quickly and coordinate with London to send us an airplane."

Omran then withdrew quickly to avoid any discussion about this issue. Badr whispered to Yusuf and Khalid, "I swear that I am worried about this strange person."

Moving away from the group and trying to light up a cigarette, Khalid said, "I learned to take care of fake lights! I see his movements fake so we should monitor him even if we fly to London after them."

Yusuf pointed to the cigarette and said, "How did you get this cigarette?"

"I couldn't help buying it from a mall during the search process," Khalid said.

He offered Yusuf a cigarette, and Badr said, "We have to get the number of the last person and call him because I agree with you that his movements are fake."

The two young men agreed with him.

\*\*\*\*

On the morning of the agreed-upon day, the private plane was waiting for them in the International Airport. The young people were walking eagerly in the abandoned airport, which itself was still an unchanged monument.

The four young men, Khalifa, Meshaal, Bibi and Omran, boarded the plane after a warm farewell from their colleagues who hanged on them the hope of achieving the dream of their homeland.

Between excitement and the anxiety, the plane closed its door and flew in the sky towards the foggy city, to find the young woman who hid the country in her *djellaba* and fled, hoping to tell them the details that no one else knew.

After the plane settled in the air, Omran received a notification from the spy program telling him that someone had used his phone. He quickly checked the pictures and found that the program took pictures of Badr and Yusuf while they were playing with the phone. He went mad. When he looked at the recently used programs, he found that the recent call file had been opened, confirming that they did not believe him, and they were certainly looking for the phone number of the man who gave him the information.

What would they plan for him? Will they go to London before him? Or will they call him and know she is in

Liverpool? How will they behave? Will they tell everyone the truth?

These questions caused him headaches and he didn't find a solution. He couldn't do anything because he was flying. He was waiting for the moment of arrival to tell Peter about what happened.

As soon as they arrived at Heathrow International Airport, Omran ran away to call Peter without being heard by anyone. Peter was happy about this call, but Omran told him that the two young men spied his system, confirming that he had no doubt that they got the phone number of the man who gave him the information. However, Peter wasn't affected by the news and only asked for the picture of the two young men. He reassured Omran that he will be the fastest person to reach the young lady.

After ending the call, Omran was in a conflict with his feelings. He had concerns that the two young men would be hurt and wished to return to his former life. However, he didn't realise that man couldn't come out of any circumstances as he was, because nothing goes back to its previous condition.

While the conspiracy was being made in the UK, the young people were missing Badr, Khalid and Yusuf. Everyone was surprised that they disappeared at once without having any information about them. Some of their colleagues volunteered to search for them and the search lasted two days, but to no avail.

How could they find the three men who travelled to London? They took advantage of the absence of security services and their colleagues' concern with Omran. The three men hid in the bag box after contacting the information investigator who told them the information Omran didn't unveil to them. This drove Badr mad and forced the other two men to board the plane secretly to catch their colleagues and save what could be saved.

As Omran and the other young people went out of Heathrow Airport to the lady's old home, Peter sent a man to hide any information about the investigator who had the address of Eugene in Liverpool. Peter didn't know that the investigator had given the young men what they wanted and they were leaving the airport heading for the nearest train station to take them to Liverpool, because they were aware that Omran was wasting their time.

Peter didn't forget to keep Eugene's house under surveillance.

****

On a quiet morning, Peter's men started watching Eugene's house, and Eugene was drinking a cup of coffee prepared by the laser system in the balcony of one of the rooms in a high-rise tower. He received a call but the caller's ID or number didn't appear on the telephone screen. Eugene knew the caller and replied with a smile, but his smile faded with the voice of the caller and remained only surprised.

He calmly ended the call and went to change his clothes. He then came out and was seriously ready to receive the disaster.

He drove a car without a plate to a place far from the downtown. He entered a small house in a semi-detached place, where he replaced the car with a small one. He then moved to the Crowne Plaza Hotel that overlooks Princes

Dock. Eugene entered the hotel to meet Atyab in one of the side rooms away from sight.

She looked at him with horror, wanting him to talk, but he kept silent for long, and said, "My heart will stop."

He took a deep breath to know what he was saying: "I received a call from London."

She steered at him, and then he said, "There are people from your country looking for you."

She sighed and said, "They must have woken up and reached the messaging machine."

He shook his head and said, "I thought this at the beginning, but there was something that raised my doubts."

She looked at him fearfully. He said, "The call was received by someone rather than the search institution. However, he was given information about you because the search was in your real name Taybah, but the employee disappeared two days after giving them the information. Thus, there is a hidden hand looking for you. The employee told them you were in Liverpool with me."

She uttered the name of her daughter aloud, but he calmed her again and said, "We shouldn't meet this period for the safety of you and your little daughter. We should communicate only through messages until we meet the young people and make sure they are from your country."

Atyab's hands trembled and her face turned yellow. Despite Eugene's attempt to keep them calm, he was worried and didn't know how to behave. It was not true the enemy would reach her after taking control of the homeland. What could it do with her after all these years?

Eugene didn't realise that the enemy didn't hold a good grip on the homeland, as there was a missing part that was in the possession of Atyab and her daughter. They had something which if the enemy got would lock the story with a steel lock.

However, our life doesn't always turn out the way we plan, as someone gets out of the way at any moment and destroys the pyramid from its base.

Peter's men saw Mrs Rachel entering Eugene's house. They told Peter quickly about this visit so that he might take action. There was something they couldn't understand, as she entered the house and came out crying after 45 minutes. No one knows that her crying because her friend Elia refused to meet her and hear her story with her adopted son.

While walking dizzy on the street, she received a call from Peter who asked her to come to his office or he would get rid of her and her son at the same time.

**London w2k**
**121 Mount St, Mayfair**

The sun was shining in the sky. Omran and the other people stood in front of the flat.

"We have now reached the house of Taybah as per the address," Omran said.

Feeling excited to meet Taybah, Bibi said, "Let's go!"

Before Khalifa rang the bell, an old woman with short white hair, came out from the next-door flat and asked them while feeling upset: "What are you doing, strangers?"

Khalifa said, "We are the relatives of Mrs Atyab."

She steered at their faces and then said, "Relatives! Don't you know that she left this house a while ago?"

"Where did she go?" Bibi asked.

She said while entering her house, "Aren't you her relatives? Communicate with her to know!"

They exchanged looks of surprise and steered at Omran, but he denied knowing this information and reassured them that he would ask again about her place. But Bibi said that as long as we have reached her house, we won't return half a step back. We will look for this information ourselves by searching inside the house.

Omran was shocked by this idea, but could not refuse, fearing to draw their attention. They broke into the house and felt that they went back in time. Despite the absence of the house's owner, the walls and furniture reflect the homeland touches here and there. In a small room, several papers were hung showing attempts to simply draw the country's landmarks and flag. The house was very small, and the search process lasted only an hour. They found nothing but the ambience of the homeland they lost.

Standing near the ladder, Bibi asked, "Didn't you find a notebook, paper or even calendar?"

The young people shook their heads and Omran said, "Although Taybah didn't empty the house of her soul, she didn't leave anything referring to her homeland. We don't know what the next step will be."

Bibi looked at Meshaal and Khalifa and said, "If you can't communicate with the person who told you that she is in London and inform him that we haven't found her, we have nothing but to return."

Omran was surprised by their quick surrender and asked for their permission to have a call.

Once he left, Bibi asked, "What do you hide?"

Khalifa smiled and said, "I feared you wouldn't understand."

She laughed and said, "Don't let me talk about my career experience and achievements!"

"I got a small, worn paper under the baby's bed," he laughed and said.

Meshaal asked Khalifa to read the message before Omran's arrival. "I don't know what is happening. My mum is worried and scared and asks Eugene to take us with him. Mum once told me that there are people who will come to take us back to our homeland. I leave you my mother's number to contact us when you read my message."

She wrote her mother's number down the paper.

Meshaal said, "It appears that her mother knows more details. We should conceal the issue from Omran; he isn't from us and not interested in our issue. We can find a solution ourselves."

"I doubt he knew that she is not here," Khalifa said.

Bibi said anxiously, "But I fear that we may fail, or the mother and her daughter face any risk. The little girl wrote my mother is worried and afraid, perhaps…"

Mashaal interrupted her and said, "We have to change our way of dealing with Omran."

His two colleagues agreed with him and left the house for the next step.

The next step was already taken by their three young colleagues who arrived in Liverpool and didn't know what to do. When they left the Liverpool Lime Street train station, Khalid suggested they should go to the address provided by the man and watch the house if the place was safe or they should call Eugene to meet him away.

Yusuf and Badr agreed to this suggestion. They got on an electronic taxi and entered the address in its display and drove safely without a driver.

They reached their destination safely. These taxis spread in mid-2021, so all developed and rich countries became in no need of drivers.

The young people liked this invention that has fixed speed and specific destination. In addition, the vehicle was comfortable and well equipped for the passengers.

The young people stopped at a sufficient distance and watched the house. Khalid noticed other men watching the place; they didn't move from their places for more than half an hour and no one came in or out of the house. They didn't know what to do.

\*\*\*\*

In a moony light, Atyab sat in the balcony of the royal suite in the hotel where she was living, while Eugene finished his phone call with Elia. The little girl Lulu was in a deep sleep.

Atiyab looked at the sky with a heart full of things that weigh the mountains, so how could a mother bear such things? Eugene apologised for interrupting her loneliness and said, "Don't worry, everything will be OK."

She smiled with satisfaction: "I am sure about that."

Before Eugene told her anything about the status quo, her phone rang but she neglected it. She didn't have a certain reason to answer. She was just afraid of the future and terrified that her daughter would be hurt.

Eugene brought her the phone and said, "Things won't be OK unless you face them."

She wiped her face with her hand and then took the phone to answer the call, "Hello."

He replied in Arabic, "Are you Taybah?"

Her face turned red and shed tears without feeling. He said, "We found your number on a paper written by your daughter and she put it under her bed in London. We need your help. You are the hope to recover our homeland. You are the missing part of the story."

She took a deep breath that terrified Eugene who was relaxing on the chair and playing with his phone. She burst into tears and couldn't say one word to the caller. Eugene took the phone after failing to calm her down. He asked the caller, "Who are you?" However, the caller insisted on talking to her, but Eugene told him that she was very upset and couldn't talk to him at that time. Eugene asked him again about his identity, and the caller said he was from Kuwait and wanted the missing part of the story which they knew nothing about its details.

Eugene ended the call and closed the phone lest he should have known her location if the call was unsafe.

After an hour of crying, she calmed down and was able to talk with him. Eugene said, "Whatever your feelings and the pressure around you, we should be more careful. You shouldn't meet them alone and must be sure of their identity in a formal way. You are still under our protection according to the recommendations of your country's authorities."

She nodded her head in approval, begging him to do this as quickly as possible because she could no longer tolerate this dissension, especially after having become sure that the young people had awakened and returned home.

He promised that he would try and left with the hope of meeting her tomorrow.

The night might have ended well, but things in front of Elia's house were not OK. Thinking of Omran made Elia unable to sleep well and he didn't know that the war was about to start. After the young people agreed to watch the house from a certain distance, Yusuf sat on the sidewalk lighting up a cigarette. He refused to wear his hat on the grounds that no one knew him in the city. Yusuf didn't know that Omran sent his picture to Peter who in turn sent it to his men.

One of Peter's men saw Yusuf and whispered in the ear of his friend asking him to make sure that the picture matched the person sitting on the sidewalk, and approached him quietly but the alarm bells sounded in his head so he looked around him to watch the two men heading to him. However, he fled without thinking.

Khalid and Badr noticed what was happening. Badr took advantage of the men's preoccupation and caught up with Yusuf, while Khalid went to the nearest telephone booth on the opposite side at the end of street. Despite the shooting, he continued to call Eugene.

Yusuf disappeared in the dark and Badr was behind the walls, while Khalid remained hidden in the telephone booth.

\*\*\*\*

Eugene was expected to return to his brother's house in midtown to meet the young people who were coming from London, but as soon as he arrived at his room in the tower, the public telephone rang and he hesitated to answer but predicted the caller and said to himself that the call might be related to Attyab.

He answered with tired voice, and the caller said, "Mr Eugene, I am Khalid and my friend's name is Badr. We will enter your home until you arrive; this is our only chance to get away from the eyes of those charged with watching your home."

He answered without hesitation, "I am coming." He might have been worried about his brother or felt curious to know the story of the men watching the house. At the same moment, Elia was fighting with Badr in the living room as he didn't know him. Khalid broke into the house and tried to end the fight, but they didn't respond to him. Elia beat his head with a baseball bat hanging on the wall, so he fell unconscious.

Badr looked at him and said, "Are you sure he didn't die?"

Khalid took the man to a nearby chair and tied him with a rope he found in a drawer. He then said, "I don't know but I hope so. Now we have to turn off the lighting so as not to draw attention and wait until Eugene arrives."

Relaxing on the couch, Badr said, "How did you know that he wasn't Eugene?"

Khalid looked at him and said, "I just called him; how can he talk to me and fight with you?"

The time went by and the sun was about to shine. Eugene entered the house cautiously, calling out to his brother. They received him calmly, and then he woke up his brother, unfastened him and let him relax on the couch in front of them.

Khalid apologised for what he had done, but Eugene's brother gave him no chance to talk and was violent in dealing with him. Eugene smiled, while Elia looked at them angrily.

"Who are you?" Eugene asked them.

Khalid and Badr told him the story from the moment they woke up and what they went through, especially as Khalid was one of the five young people who visited big Island. They went on talking until they reached the issue of Omran who came calmly, got angry, left suddenly, and then came back peacefully, which raised their doubts. They watched him and took the phone number of the man who provided them with information about Attyab, which Omran hid for no clear reason.

They flew with their friend Yusuf, who was chased by unknown men, and as soon as they arrived at Heathrow Airport, they boarded a train and came here according to the address they had.

Eugene asked, "Do you have other colleagues in London?"

Badr said, "Yes, Mr Omran."

Elia stood up calmly, opened his phone and extended his hand to them. "Is this Omran you can see in the picture?"

They exchanged looks and nodded, confirming that he was Omran.

Elia came to tell them the truth and recount the story of Omran, including Peter's threats and rejection of Omran's invention and how Omran came to the dead country.

Badr got angry when he heard the term of the 'dead country' and asked him to respect his country. Elia called it 'the country that is in a coma'. Then he tried to calm Badr down in order to benefit from this important meeting.

Elia went on recounting the story and told them about the way he got the information about his friend. Dr Leva bribed one of Peter's secretaries to reveal the hidden secrets of Mrs Rachel and Omran. He told them that he was the son of Dr Salem whose picture was shown up on the system.

Elia stopped to take a sigh of relief and they were eagerly awaiting him to continue his talk.

He said, "Unfortunately, with the help of a psychiatrist, Omran's memory was erased after his parents were killed. He then was adopted by Rachel, so he can't belong to you."

Khalid and Badr became increasingly concerned about his companions in London.

However, he was reassured that Attyab received a call from one of them last night, and she asked them to come to Liverpool. However, they had to be more cautious about Omran and the men around the house. They were asked to sit at home and never leave. He would even go to meet Attyab and receive those coming from London to discover the unknown parts of the issue because sending Omran to the young people in London while knowing she wasn't there meant that her life was in danger and even their lives if they insisted on coming here.

After this talk, Elia went to prepare a snack for the two young men. Eugene went out to meet Attyab and did not notice the car that was following him. Not all the men left behind Yusuf. They saw Eugene entering the room. Peter ordered them to identify his destination.

The sun shone and Omran woke up. He spent the last night with the young people in a restaurant after asking him for a little bit of fun before returning home. They then returned home in Hammersmith in early morning.

Omran was surprised by the absence of the young people in the house. He asked himself, "Where they could be?" He didn't think that they were on their way to Liverpool and thought that they might have been gone for shopping with Bibi. After the train had arrived at the Liverpool Lime Street railway station, the young people got off and called Attyab from the telephone booth at the station, but her phone was shut off since yesterday.

They exchanged looks, awaiting a solution from each other. Bibi said, "Let's eat so we can think well!"

Khalifa looked at her and said, "How can we get money?"

She smiled and said, "From Omran's wallet."

Upon seeing the two young men supersized, Bibi said, "What's wrong with you? I didn't steal the money from him; I borrowed it from him when he was under anaesthetic before he slept."

"I don't like this method, but it is good for our situation. This at least will slow down his steps to catch up with us," Meshaal said while walking.

They went on the streets in search of suitable restaurants. They were stopped by Bibi who shouted, "It's Yusuf."

Meshaal shouted at her, "Why would Yusuf come here?"

She insisted that the one whom she saw was Yusuf, and then she ran away from them to catch up with the man. He took off his hat and showed that he was Yusuf. However, Yusuf was surprised and hugged Khalifa and Meshaal. Meshaal drove him away and asked him, "What brought you here?"

Yusuf turned right and left and then took them to a famous restaurant. They sat out of sight, and Yusuf recounted the story from the beginning. He told them that Badr and Khalid were in his house and he had been hunted without knowing the reason. If he couldn't hide himself until the morning, he would be in their grip.

Meshaal said, "We have to go to the house about which Yusuf is talking."

They agreed and went to watch the situation from afar.

Omran went crazy while walking around the streets. It was 3:00 p.m. and no one had ever heard of them. He received a call from Peter asking him when they would return and leave the country because he had located Eugene and would put his hand on the damned girl soon.

Omran sat in a bus station and said to him, "Peter, I can't find them. I have been looking for them more than three hours ago."

He then asked him to come to Liverpool as soon as possible as they would move there. Peter's suspicions were confirmed when Omran asked some money from him for losing his wallet.

Omran ended the call and didn't believe that those who were on the top of innocence and purity would plan with the precision that made him not pay attention or doubt anything.

****

In Elia's house, where they felt calm before the storm, Elia was very nervous. He walked around the salon and looked from the window from time to time, while Khalid and Badr searched the Internet for some details about their country, but they found nothing as all information go back to early 2018. No one spoke of what they had gone through as if someone had deliberately hidden such information.

They stood up upon hearing the doorbell ring. "It may be Eugene," Badr said.

Elia said, "No, Eugene knows the password." He opened the door screen to see the pizza vendor and told him that they didn't order pizza, asking him to leave. However, the pizza vendor kept ringing the bell. Elia opened the door angrily, and tried to box the man, but he received a strong box which drove him away from the door. The man and his friend broke into the house.

They discovered that it was Yusuf and Khalifah. Elia wanted to attack, but Khalid and Badr drove him away. "He is our friend." The doorbell rang again, and Yusuf opened the door to allow Meshaal and Bibi in. He apologised for his behaviour as they were afraid of drawing attention as was happened yesterday.

Elia felt that his house was broken, and he wanted to expel them all, but he breathed a sigh of relief and called his brother to come quickly.

Eugene's phone rang while driving his car to the small house. He answered the call of his brother and didn't notice that there was a car watching him since the morning. Eugene came to the house by a motorcycle. Elia was still on the line telling him that the young people arrived from London. He then ended the call while feeling angry that his brother didn't interact with him.

Eugene arrived at the hotel and Peter's men followed him cautiously until they identified the room of Attyab. They then briefed Peter on this information. He said to them, "Catch her quietly and bring her to me in the office."

They were four men; two of them stayed in the hotel cellar and the other two went up to stay on the same floor.

Meanwhile, Eugene was in her suite trying to convince her to come with him to meet the young people. However, she refused irrationally and said: "It isn't me who will meet the young people, but my daughter."

The young girl hugged her mum as she sat on the chair in the centre of the room, saying, "I won't leave you for a moment."

Attyab hugged her daughter and let the little princess sit on her lap. "Baby, it is the time to go back to your homeland."

The daughter kept crying and said, "You are my homeland, Mum."

Attyab caught her little daughter from her shoulder and handed her to Eugene who was standing by the window. "If you attend, tell them the whole story, but if you can't, hand my baby and tell them that the homeland has become in their hands."

Eugene screamed angrily, "Why?"

Wiping her tears, Attyab said, "Didn't you say that your brother's house is being watched? Didn't you tell me that Omran is Elia's friend? Didn't you say that the young people arrived from London?"

"Yes," Eugene said.

She said, "All attention is directed to me, and my little daughter should be safely handed to the young people."

The little princess took her mum's hand and asked her to sit on the floor, saying, "Mum, promise me to be OK."

The mum hugged her and said, "I promise you as much as I can."

Attyab then brought a small back bag and put her daughter in it. She asked Eugene to carry the bag and leave the hotel safely.

Eugene agreed to Attyab's request and the girl surrendered to her mother's orders. They actually came out of the suite quietly to where the motorcycle was waiting.

When the men were assured that Eugene moved away, they broke into the suite as expected and asked her to go with them calmly.

Everyone was moving to his destiny. Attyab got on the car and didn't know whom she would meet. Meanwhile, the little girl was about to be suffocated inside the bag. Omran boarded the train towards the unknown, and Rachel was confused and didn't know what to do to save her son from Peter's megalomania.

\*\*\*\*

When love moves us with its strength, miracles are created from our depths. One of the most painful feelings is when you can't reassure those hearts waiting for your return with a great victory, because you aren't satisfied with your abilities to face the coming challenges.

Feeling worried and terrified, Bibi unveiled what she was thinking of. "Omran is coming to us." However, no one replied to her, and they kept silent until five o'clock. Elia decided to contact his brother because he was very worried about him. As Eugene entered with a pale face, his brother rushed to him, asking about the reason for his delay and the exhaustion that turned his face pale.

However, Eugene didn't answer and sat down on a long armchair. He carefully took off the bag from his back, opened it and got the girl out amid the astonishment of all people.

"Is this Attyab?" Yusuf asked while feeling shocked.

Eugene shook his head and then asked them to bring him water.

Elia hurried to fetch the water, and Eugene gave it to the little girl, but she refused to drink and clung more to his arm. After drinking, Eugene said, "This is the daughter of Attyab and she asked me to bring her to you. If she is able to escape, she will come and tell you what to do, or the little girl is your homeland. With the appearance of the first sign of danger, please take her and go back to your country quickly."

"I don't understand how the girl can be our homeland," said Badr.

Eugene shook his head and said, "I also don't understand; the events are taking place like a cloud raining with anger, and the police don't know who is behind all these events."

Bibi moved towards Lulu and started playing and talking so the little girl could reassure her about Attyab whom she didn't know anything about.

The striving mother who deserves a golden memento arrived at a dark basement. They parked the car and got her out with a ribbon tied on her eyes in preparation for meeting the beast after a moment. Attyab didn't know what was waiting for her, but she believed that she would face everything bravely. She talked with herself that everything would end, and she would come back to her homeland.

Attyab felt entering a very cold room after getting out of the elevator. The man accompanying her said: "Sit here until my master comes."

She asked him, "Could you remove the ribbon from my eyes and untie my hands?"

"We have orders to deal with you with caution," said the man. "You are people with precedents in resistance and ability to overcome crises."

"With all pride, O bad person," she whispered with her mother tongue.

The man didn't understand what she said and didn't have the curiosity to know. He sat her on a chair and went silently. Three minutes passed as if she spent her whole life with misery. She heard the sound of the door creak and persons approaching her. Attyab was afraid that things would turn away from what she had predicted. However, she was brave to maintain her calm.

The person who entered the room was insistent on keeping silent, leaving her confused, and the minutes passed…

"I think you're a woman," Attyab said to the person who was sitting with her in the room.

She didn't hear an answer, and despite the coldness of the room, her forehead was sweating. "Why are you silent? Your estrogen is very high, and it is good that you are so. I am aware of this issue; we are women like each other."

However, she didn't hear any answer, and she wanted to hear anything to know that she was on the right track.

Attyab said, "You have distinguished fragrance; the fragrance of your motherhood."

She heard the breath of motherhood from the person sitting in front of her, so she was filled with joy for the first time in seven years. Attyab said, "Do you have a son or a daughter? It appears that you haven't seen him for a while."

113

She then heard the tortured voice of Rachel, "You are right; I am a woman, but not a mother. I suffer from uterus deformity, which prevents me from giving birth to a child."

"You mightn't give birth but adopt a child," said Attyab with a smile. "This is clear from the tenderness of your voice."

Rachel tried to change the topic: "I see you are talking confidently; aren't you afraid that I may harm you?"

"We are mothers and you won't hurt me because you know the meaning of orphan hood in the lives of children." Attyab laughed loudly despite her need to cry loudly.

Rachel shed tears silently and wiped them with her hand. She then left the place quickly in order not to be impacted by Attyab's words that were full of confidentiality.

Rachel fled to Peter's office and didn't know what to say but decided to convince him of allowing his hostage to go back to her daughter, even if the price was to unveil her secret to Omran. She was ready to do her best to regain her son's heart, even if she moved with him to his motherland.

Rachel was about to break into the office but stopped when she heard the voice of his son inside. She wanted to know what was going on.

Peter was talking with Omran about the young people fleeing London to Liverpool, and Peter began to mourn her son in a harsh tone, which angered her. However, she was amazed that Omran surrendered, obeyed him and sold himself and humanity to him. Rachel went away in order to not to distract the attention, and looked from behind a wall to see Peter heading towards the hostage. Omran went outside as if he was a person she didn't know.

Omran left the building and felt that he had gone into a wide space where he had no shelter. He chose to go to his house and meet his mother, but he held his head with both hands to come him back to his senses. He remembered that he still had some negative feelings towards her so he decided to visit his friend Elia, especially as they haven't met for a long time and this would be a good opportunity to apologise for the long absence. He thought that Elia wouldn't hesitate to accept his apology if he explained his circumstances. He got on an electronic taxi and headed for Elia's house, changing things without warning.

When the marine environment settles, the shipmaster knows that this will not last and he must take precautions against the coming storm. This was what Meshaal was thinking of, while looking at the wall clock; it was 8:30 p.m. He looked at the sleeping princess and said, "What is the guilt of this child?"

"His only sin is that she is the daughter of a brave mother," Khalifa replied, rubbing her black hair with his hands.

He sat next to the girl and Khalifa, saying, "This calm doesn't please me; my heart confirms that we will face a disaster."

The doorbell rang, and Badr said sarcastically as he came from the kitchen with Bibi carrying a glass of juice, "We had faced the disaster, my friend."

Elia looked at the screen and laughed because it saw Omran's face. He rushed to tell the young people and asked them to go upstairs. They asked with confusion, "Who is coming?"

He said to them nervously, "It is Omran."

They went upstairs quickly as if they were fleeing from a pandemic, leaving the girl sleeping on the couch. However, Bibi drew their attention, so Khalifah rushed to carry her.

Elia stood in front of the door, picking up his breath and turning to reassure himself that nothing was striking. He opened the door as he tried to ignore his anger.

Elia stood in front of the door while taking a sigh of relief and looking behind to make sure that nothing would draw attention. He opened the door while trying to hide his anger.

Looking at each other, Omran rushed to hug his friend and Elia hugged him warmly in order to not to let Omran doubt him. Omran went to the salon, asking him about his news and what had happened with him throughout his absence. Omran relaxed on his favourite couch and said: "You should order pizza for dinner as we were doing in the past. Talk to me this evening about what you did in my absence."

Elia was distracted and confused for the presence of the young people, but Omran explained that he was upset by the last call with Elia. "Elia, I am sorry for ignoring your calls, but if I tell you my severe circumstances, you will certainly excuse me."

Elia did not answer and preferred to remain silent again.

In an attempt to let Elia talk, Omran asked, "How is Dr Leva?

Elia smiled. "She moved to the US to participate in a research."

Omran hit his shoulder and said, "And your heart, my friend?"

Elia smiled and said, "If you mean the beats of love, it awaits you as agreed; otherwise it beats every day as optimistic as the sun shines every morning spreading hope."

Omran was surprised by his friend's reply and didn't understand anything. He took out his phone to order pizza for dinner but ended the call upon hearing the door crack.

Before asking Elia about the coming, he heard, "Eugene arrived, will you welcome him?"

Omran stopped in surprise and looked at Elia as if he was waiting for an explanation. Eugene was frozen when he saw Omran in the centre of the house. Elia breathed a sigh of relief and said, "This is my brother Eugene and this is my friend Omran."

\*\*\*\*

What a strange world! You hide what we are looking for and unveil what we are fleeing from. Peter couldn't resist Attyab's silence. He sat in front of her for more than an hour, asking, enforcing and threatening her. However, she didn't respond to him and kept silent with confidence.

He was agitated like boiling water and took off the ribbon from her eyes so the visual communication would bring a little bit of shudder to her heart.

After taking off the lace, Attyab's wide eyes shone with the long eyelashes that were like the peacock feathers. She looked at him with strength, confidence and defiance, and he stood rigidly in front of her.

He turned his eyes away from her and said, "I wouldn't have hurt you unless you hide something related to me."

She looked at him admiringly. "I don't know you to hide something related to you. Have we met before?"

She took a deep breath and said, "Where do you hide the blue cells?"

She smiled and answered his question, "To arrest them in the virtual world?"

He answered involuntarily, "Yes…I mean, no…not exactly."

She tilted her head forward and told him to come closer. He approached without hesitation: "Death is easier for me than ending my homeland's fate with both hands."

His face turned red and said, "I will kill your daughter."

Attyab hid her fear and showed her courage between her provocative laughs. "Do whatever you want; your father's life will inevitably end at the moment of ending my daughter's life."

Peter got confused and approached from her, whispering, "What do you know about my father?"

"Do you think we are people who don't know anything about their homeland?" she said while smiling.

Peter shook his head as if he was rejecting ideas and feelings seizing him. He then said provocatively, "You will give me the cells; do you understand? Or…"

She challenged him, saying, "Or you will kill me as Rachel did with Dr Salem?"

He was surprised at the information she had and left the room without saying one word. Peter knew that he had lost in this conversation and that she knew more than he thought. He came out of the building, breathing with difficulty and trying to arrange his ideas for what he wanted. However, he didn't notice that Rachel was watching him from the window and was surprised by his condition.

Peter's condition was unstable.

Omran knew that Eugene was the only man who knew the place of Attyab, without knowing that her daughter was with him in the same house. Throughout this time, he was persuading Eugene to tell him about the place of the woman and her daughter to end this torment and return to his former life.

The young people were on the threshold, listening to the conversation between the three men downstairs, without paying attention to Lulu, who was also listening to their comments and analysis of the events. "Shouldn't we have taken step to change our situation? What have you felt while running away like criminals?"

"You are ready to seize any chance. In fact, we were not prepared for the chance to meet Omran and confront him. We are only thinking about how to escape."

They heard the little girl saying: "But I am ready for this."

The young people saw the girl descending and crossing through them. They tried to catch her but she was faster than them.

She stood in front of the three young men downstairs, screaming with her innocent voice at the young man whom she saw selfish and didn't care for anyone.

"Don't lie to him and tell the truth; I am Lulu, the daughter of Attyab for whom you are searching. I'm in front of you, what will you do?" the little girl said.

Omran was shocked and exchanged looks with Elia and Eugene. Omran said, "My mother always says that we lose part of our personality after any experience we have, and then we experience something else. Even if you win this battle, are you going back to what you were?" she said.

Lulu was screaming madly, her forehead was sweating and her body trembled as she stood in front of Omran. Eugene tried to calm the child down and reassure her that nothing would hurt her or Attyab.

Yusuf whispered to the young people, "I am ashamed of myself; the little girl stands before Omran, and we are hiding here."

Mashaal shook his head in support of his words. "Come on, young people."

They all went down to the saloon, to be another shock for Omran. He sat down as he wasn't able to stand.

Before anyone uttered any word or Omran commented, the child fell unconscious in Eugene's hands, her breath were accelerating in a terrifying way. They were all afraid and Eugene carried her without thinking to the nearest hospital. It wasn't reasonable to lose the child after being kept by her mother all these years.

It was almost the midnight and the girl was still in the ICU. They all were standing outside, feeling worried. Elia looked at his friend and said, "Why are you still here?"

Omran was surprised by his question: "You are my friend, why do you ask me this question?"

"To tell Peter the news; call him now and tell him," Elia said.

Eugene pointed to Omran, asking him to keep silent and drove him away to drink a cup of coffee. As soon as the two walked away, three doctors came out of Lulu's room and said to the young people, "Who can we talk to?"

All of them turned to Meshaal and asked him to catch up with them.

In the office, when he sat in front of the three doctors, they asked him about what he knew about the child and her mother. Meshaal was confused and didn't know what to say. One of them said, "Sorry, we have to report to the police. The girl's life is in danger," one of the doctors said.

Meshaal's face turned pale but was calmed down by the entrance of Eugene. The latter showed them his official identity card and asked them not to report to the police. He also told them that he was officially mandated to manage the mother and daughter's affairs, with the support of the British government and the Security Council.

The doctors kept silent, and the oldest one of them said, "Mr Eugene, the child's condition is very dangerous."

Amid the anxiety of Eugene and Meshaal, the doctor said: "There are cells planted in her body that endanger her life, and they must be removed immediately."

"They are certainly the blue cells," Meshaal said.

Eugene said, as if he was remembering something, "That's why she used to say that her daughter is homeland."

Meshaal said, "We have to hide the matter from Omran; will you tell her mother?"

"I can't reach her, and the hotel staff says she left at the moment I left the hotel."

The doctor interrupted them, saying, "Pardon, what have you decided? The child;s life is in danger."

"Doctor, carry out the operation, but keep child healthy," Eugene said.

The doctor asked them to sign the operation documents to be responsible for the operation seriousness. Then they tried to keep Omran away from the place, but he was like a stubborn child not responding.

**You don't know how the mercy comes down to you from the heaven. After six hours, one of the doctors went out of the operation room to tell them that the operation succeeded and the child's condition was stable. The young people prostrated to thank god, and the doctor said, "The cells are ready to be delivered."

"Which cells?" Omran said with amazement.

Khalid said sarcastically, "Cancer cells."

The doctor went away, asking them to be calm. Omran started asking Eugene, but Badr snubbed him. "I think it is enough of you to remain unwanted and annoying us with your curiosity. We won't tell you."

"I just want to be in the picture," Omran said.

Meshaal said sarcastically, "I will believe that you want to be in the picture, but not to inform your master of the news. We will receive the blue cells that we and you are looking for. We and your master will fight for them. Are you now in the picture?"

Omran expressed his surprise and asked for more information. The nurse ended this fight and told them that they could see the child individually. They rushed to the room, leaving Omran behind them. At this moment, he received a call from Peter, and, as the young people expected, Omran informed him of what happened at Elia's house.

Peter smiled and said, "Wonderful, go away from the young people and watch the child's room. I will send men to take the child from her bed."

Omran got afraid. "What do you want from the child? You want the cells, and I will fetch them for you."

Peter smiled horribly and said, "To return her to her mother."

Omran ended the call but didn't believe what he heard. He had a strange feeling, so he called his mother Rachel, but she didn't answer. It was the first time she didn't answer his call.

When we lose hope of communicating with one of them, we become other persons.

****

Amid the flux of events and when we sink in calamities, we have to make sure that there are some people who love us despite the geographical distances that separate us. Elia received a call while going out of the hospital with Khalifa and Badr. He looked at the phone and then apologised for moving away.

He answered the phone saying, "You are better than a cup of cold water to drink in the summer."

She laughed and said, "Should I call you in order to not to ignore me, man?"

He took a deep breath and said, "My dear Leva, I am facing a problem and I don't know its beginning and end; what is funny is that it broke into my life. I hope you are beside me."

He started revealing to her the concerns caused by Omran, as well as the problem of the little girl and her lost mother, while she tried to calm him down. Then she said jokingly: "I fear that I come back from the US and find your hair turned white, Doctor."

He laughed and said, "If you find hair at all."

Her laugh touched his feelings, and he thanked her for calling him, and hoped that she would return soon.

He didn't know where to go from the joy. He felt as if he was flying while heading towards Khalifa and Badr in the cafe opposite the hospital.

As far as Elia was full of joy, the concern gripped his brother's heart after failing to reach Attyab. Once he proved that Omran and his master were behind Attyab's disappearance as he noticed a strange movement around the child's room, he rushed to the suspect man because this gang would seize any chance to hurt the little girl. He asked her doctor to issue a permission to leave the hospital. Although the doctor explained to him how much she needed medical care during this period, he insisted that her presence at home was safer than the hospital.

He took her out with a medical escort to his brother's house and called the police to surround the house until the young people would leave Liverpool.

Of course, this step hindered the conspiracy of Peter and Omran, who paved the way for this. At the lunch table, Omran felt that he was being treated badly, but he didn't care. If he couldn't take the kid, he would certainly take the cells. While thinking of the robbery plan, Omran was interrupted by Bibi's saying that she wanted to go to the beauty salon and Yusuf wanted to go shopping. They all were amazed at their requests. At the same time, there was no justification for rejection. Elia told Bibi about the location of the nearest salon and asked to accompany Yusuf to the market. Meshaal and Khalifa became nervous. They did something incomprehensible, especially as Bibi insisted on accompanying Badr on the grounds that the local saloons were mixed. He tried to understand something, but he could only allow Khalifa to go out to the cafe until the others came back because Eugene wanted to sleep and this would be a good opportunity to be beside the little girl after Omran decided to visit Rachel.

****

Peter stood behind the glass of the ICU unit, contemplating the body of his father who had been sleeping on the bed for more than eight years. At this very moment, Peter was stripped of his pride and retuned a little child contemplating the window and waiting for his father to return. He shed tears that cleaned his inner being and brought him back to his life.

"Mr Peter!" said the doctor of his father.

Peter looked at him after wiping his tears: "Did my father's condition improve?"

The doctor shook his head, saying, "No…It has been the same since eight years ago."

Peter sighed and said, "You haven't found a cure for his condition throughout these years."

"Mr Peter, you know what your father suffers from – erosion in the internal organs – and the age diseases are very critical, and it is difficult to find a cure. What do you think of finding a solution and providing alternative treatment? I told you from the moment you entered the hospital that your father needs to implant electronic cells," the doctor said.

Peter cried out angrily, "I brought you hundreds of them."

"You came with hundreds of them, and we made four operations for your father in one year, but none of them succeeded, because we need a certain type of cells – the blue human cells – which you haven't brought so far," the doctor said.

He hit his fist on the wall. "I burned a whole country, scattered families, dispersed loved ones, and got nothing, but I will get what I need soon."

At the same moment, he received a call from Omran telling him joyfully that he got the electronic cells that had been removed from the child as he managed to steal them from the house in the absence of the young people. Peter laughed aloud and hugged the doctor involuntarily. He ordered Omran to come immediately to the hospital to start the operation. Peter sent him the coordinates and ordered him to shut off his phone so that no one could know his location.

Amid Omran's strong joy, he arrived at the hospital carrying the box of electronic cells and handed it to Peter, with a broad smile painted on his face. Peter opened the box to see the cells and then went to the doctor, saying, "I trust you, Doctor. This is the moment we have been waiting for years."

The doctor smiled and assured him that everything would be fine. He entered the operating room carrying his great hope.

The medical staff has spent more than two hours in the operation room. After the doctors had succeeded in implanting four cells in the body, they started implanting others in the heart. The nurse said, "Doctor!"

The doctor looked at him intently, and the nurse stretched out his hand to show him that the gloves turned blue. The nurse said, "It seems that the cells are fake."

They checked the other two cells in the box as they were dyed professionally, but the temperature of the room revealed the trick. What would they do? What would they say to Peter? What was the fate of the body? What about the implanted cells? What was the fate of the young man who came with the cells?

The time stopped in the operation room and each one asked the other with his eyes for the right solution.

\*\*\*\*

**7:00 p.m.**

In Elia's house, Eugene was roaming the place angrily, denouncing their delay to this time. They came back at 7:30 p.m., and he shouted at them, "Omran's phone is shut off and the cell box is lost."

The young people's faces have changed, and Meshaal ran towards the rooms looking for the box but found nothing. He became angry and wanted to shout at Bibi because she was the one who insisted that everyone should have left.

However, she said before he become kindled with anger, "Let him take the box, and let him and his master go to hell!"

Eugene asked her: "What do you mean?"

She raised her ten fingers in the air, saying: "Because the truth is hidden here, under my artificial nails. I insisted on leaving the house to let him take the false cells that are dyed like my nails so we can't see his miserable face."

Khalifa asked her: "What have you put in the box?"

Bibi told them that she had taken some cells from the old weapon shop and dyed them after seeing Omran's insistence in the hospital to accompany them, even though he knew that everyone had known his plan.

Eugene said: "But I am worried about Attyab. If he knows that the cells are fake, he will harm her. You should leave Liverpool tonight as Peter and Omran won't let the matter pass peacefully."

Elia said, "I suggest we go to the nearest train station and fly from there to any destination where you can arrange to return home."

Badr looked at him. "Will you come with us?"

"I want to see this nation you are defending," he smiled enthusiastically.

All of them agreed with him, and Eugene asked them to leave as quickly as possible. They went to the nearest railway station on Liverpool Lime Street, and then they headed to Bristol Temple Meads railway station.

They – the young people, the child and Elia – all boarded the train, but Eugene retreated, saying, "I will bring Attyab and come after you."

The train ran fast, and Elia shouted, "My god, I forgot my phone on the charger at home."

"This is better than Omran follows you," Khalid said to him.

\*\*\*\*

Eugene went back home thinking how he could find Attyab without endangering her. As soon as he entered the house, he started thinking of the promise he gave to the child until he heard the phone ring. He tried to disregard it in the beginning, but he couldn't. It wasn't his phone, but the phone that was connected to the charger. He knew it was Elia's phone.

"Elia, how irresponsible you are!" He looked at the screen with curiosity about the identity of the caller. However, the number wasn't visible on the screen.

Eugene answered the call, "Hello…Who speaks?…I am Eugene, the elder brother of Elia…"

\*\*\*\*

**At dawn (3:15 a.m.)**

In the hospital, Peter fell asleep on his chair in front of the operation room, while Omran was going back and forth, looking at the clock hanged at the corridor.

Peter woke up and said, "Didn't anyone come out to reassure us?"

"No one," Omran said.

After half an hour, the doctor came out with his head down. Peter stood in front of him with trembling feet. "Doctor, how is my father?" Peter asked.

The doctor looked at Omran to read his facial expressions and know whether he was honest or not, and whether he brought the cells by mistake or wanted to keep Peter silent and give him only hope.

He said to them: "Sorry, the operation failed."

Peter and Omran asked him at the same time: "How?"

"It seems that someone has put fake cells in the box and thank god that we noticed that before implanting them in the heart. We removed the cells we have implanted," the doctor said.

Peter cried out from his depths, saying, "I hate you all."

He didn't know that the time was too late, and the immigrant bird was now flying home after the facilities he obtained from Bristol.

Omran and Peter arrived at Elia's house and found it empty of any features of life. The house was dark, and no one responded to the doorbell. Omran asked, "Will we break into the house?"

Peter said to him, "Break into the house, and I will go to Attyab. This is my last trump card."

Omran broke a window and jumped into the house. Then he heard the police cars roaring up on the quiet street. They cordoned off the place and took Omran with them for illegally breaking into the house.

This scene brought terror to Peter's heart, making him go quickly to his victim. He arrived there at dawn to find Rachel sitting calmly in his office drinking coffee. He ignored her and completed his journey of looking for Attyab. He got crazy when he found the room empty with no guards. He returned to Rachel to shout at her.

She replied calmly: "The fellow told me that you had ordered him to move her out of Liverpool."

He shouted more, "I didn't give any orders to anyone…I will kill you all…"

He cried hysterically, and Rachel was looking at him helplessly.

\*\*\*\*

The morning sun shone to end the darkness of the night and its tragedies and pains. We should always have strong hope that God will have mercy on us and revive our life.

Despite all ordeals, the young people sat quietly on the beach before the tall towers. They hoped that day would be better than the previous one.

Nour said: "We have waited long without achieving any results, and we have to travel to London."

"You are right, but how can we travel without having the means?" Mohammed said.

Salman asked who was next to him: "Did you see what I see?"

Abu Mubarak was surprised. "Where?"

"I see the youthful spectrum," Salman shouted.

The young people turned and watched with caution. They weren't ready to be disappointed again.

The plane flew from Bristol and landed on Falk Island and crossed the Gulf water through the tunnel linking the island to the beach. The young people met each other, and started crying, hugging and kissing the heads of each other. In addition, they prostrated to thank God, but were sad for the absence of Khalid, Badr and Yusuf.

They then became quiet and went around the newcomers to know the details as they were thirsty to hear the story.

He asked Abdul Aziz, "You left with Omran, and came back with two new persons...What happened? What is the story?"

Meshaal answered as if he remembered something, "Right, this is Elia, the friend of Omran, the brother of Eugene, and the fellow of Attyab and her daughter. This is also Lulu, the hero Lulu."

They turned their attention to the child so she hid behind Bibi while suffering from the pain of the operation. Nawar asked in surprise, "Where is Attyab?"

Khalid changed the topic, saying, "Friends, can we have a rest? What we went through was very bitter. Let's breathe a sigh of relief and we promise to tell you the details."

They went to a nearby hotel, and it was a good chance for the child to adapt to the new place. Badr remained introducing some friends to Elia.

\*\*\*\*

At sunset, they returned to meet on the beach. Mohammad and other persons provided them with speakers and microphones to know the details of what happened to them.

Khalifa recounted the story from the moment they arrived at London-based Heathrow Airport until they entered Attyab's house and got a small message under the bed. He also told them about their communication with Attyab and Eugene, as well as their plan to hide all issues from Omran for doubting his credibility.

Meanwhile, Khalid told them about his doubts with his friends before traveling and after the phone was stolen. He also told them that they moved from London Airport to the Liverpool railway station to get the address from the investigator through the phone. Then they broke into Elia's house. Khalid gave a broad smile to Elia who was sitting among the young people.

Bibi told them about Eugene's help and the child's meeting with Omran with all bravery, revealing that the cells were implanted in her body. She added that the child went through a dangerous operation and that they evaded Omran and came here with the help of Bristol team.

"But I don't know where my mother is now. She told me she would be OK, but I don't know how to assure her," the little daughter said.

Bibi hugged her before shedding tears, and said, "Eugene would certainly assure her."

Bibi then removed the artificial nails with the help of the girls to get out the blue cells. She gave them to Mohammed, the leader of the group, and said to him, "This is my nation."

Mohammad took the cells but didn't know what to do. He said, "How could we benefit from them? Their details are still missing…"

"Could you let me to narrate the missing details?" Manal said.

She stood in front of the young people and told them the missing details. The surprise was the man and the woman standing next to her. The child screamed madly, "She is my mother." She jumped to hug her with passion, safely and love.

Amid the young people's surprise, Elia hugged his brother and the young expatriates turned around him. Yusuf and Khalid asked, "How have you come?" The phone rang in Eugene's pocket and he took it out and gave to Elia, saying, "It's your phone, you forgot it in Liverpool."

In the hustle and bustle of events, Elia answered the phone, "Hello, Leva!"

"What do you think of my surprise for your birthday?" Leva asked him.

He looked at his brother in astonishment: "But how?"

"I don't have time, so let Eugene explain to you. I just liked to say I'm with you despite the distances that separate us, Elia," Leva said.

Elia didn't know what to answer. He ended the call and the smile was still painted on his face. The young people turned around the two new guests again.

Eugene said, "After bidding farewell to you at the train station, I returned home confused about how to help Attyab go back to her daughter. While I was drowning in thinking, the phone rang but I ignored. However, it kept ringing, and I knew that it was Elia's phone. I was curious to answer as the number didn't appear on the screen. It was Leva from the US and she wanted to talk but I told her that I am Eugene and not Elia. However, she asked for the coordinates of our house in order to reach Attyab safely after getting released from the confinement of Peter who accepted the bribe and leaked information about Omran. As soon as she arrived, we boarded a private plane and came here so that Peter couldn't pursue her."

Eugene didn't tell them that he had called the police to watch the house and thwart the planned incursion, respecting Elia's feelings.

Hugging her daughter, Attyab said, "We have been here since morning, but we were wandering. We didn't know the destination after leaving the airport. At the end, Allah sent us this beautiful girl who guided us to this place. I can't believe that this nightmare is over."

She burst into tears, and the girls hugged her until she calmed down.

Attyab started narrating the story and the missing part…

"Dr Salem had invented a car transferring the passengers from a place to another without a change in time in late 2017. The invention spread in early 2018, and it was above all hypotheses and theories that are represented in the fact that the individual has the ability to move from a place to another without losing part of his memory. Suddenly, anonymous entities attacked Dr Salem although his invention spread in my country and some neighbouring countries. He also received threats to stop this invention despite its spread. However, Dr Salem refused because of finding no reason to stop his invention that represented a qualitative leap in the country's scientific history – as you know.

After two months of attacking the invention, the motherboard was hacked by Internet hackers. Thus, Dr Salem lost control of the car programming, and then we started to lose the car users one after another without a logical reason or obvious defect. After investigations, it was found that motherboard hackers tampered with the digital programming of cars. They also began to withdraw the energy from the cars. Thus, if someone gets on them, he moves into the virtual world without. The electronic cells in the car panels turn blue because the human cells entered in their structure.

We couldn't do anything and the people got terrified. Dr Salem was assassinated after unveiling the invention secrets, which enforced me to implant these cells in my daughter's cells. We fled to London and asked for protection until we could meet the enemy. The enemy wasn't known at that time."

Badr said, "The only thing that remained unknown is the reaction of Omran and Peter."

Eugene changed the topic again. "Won't you return the cells to their places to end the situation?"

All of them supported him before the occurrence of something that would hinder ending the crisis. The young people were divided into several groups, and each group stood at a selected area awaiting those returning from the virtual world. Mohammed, Meshaal and Khalifah, Attyab, Eugene, Elia, Bibi and the child moved to Dr Salem's lab in the scientific club, where Attyab would show them the motherboard in one of the secret rooms which Dr Salem informed her of its location as if he knew that she would guide people to it when needed. He had recorded his message that appeared to the young people during the search.

Although it was midnight, the unveiled secrets were like the shining sun in the night darkness. The car beam rose to the sky, indicating that those who were absent in the virtual world came back to the real world. Although the young people were happy, they shed tears and fell prostrate to God. The returnees included Suhaib who was terrified of what happened. Osman shouted, "Dr Ahmed Nabil said, 'the end is worth waiting', and it is really worth it."

Just as the scene of their success and the return of everyone were beyond description, what Rachel saw was also beyond her endurance as she saw Peter after he had committed suicide in his office.

Rachel came out calmly from the office and didn't call the ambulance, but her phone rang to get another shock. She answered with her sweet voice, "Hello, Rachel speaking."

The caller said, "Madam, I am Officer Steven from the Liverpool Police Station. We have arrested your son Omran. I hope you come with a lawyer upon his request because Mr Shaman doesn't answer our calls."

"I am an infertile woman and have no children," she answered.

Rachel ended the call and threw the phone at the nearest container. She went to the airport building to travel where she intended to start a new life.